The Boy Who Knew Too Much

Anthony Winnall

First edition 2023

Cover illustration by Anna Molineux
Additional illustrations by Erin Wildboar

ISBN 9798866519866

The book could not have been done without the help of:
Heather Flack, Anna Molineux, Kieren Molineux, Liz Munslow, Erin Wildboar, Olivia Winnall, Rosemary Winnall, Simon Winnall

CHAPTER 1

Freddie Windsor was an ordinary sort of boy. Granted a fairly lucky sort of boy, after all he had survived a World War and so did most of his family and so did his dad. Some boys by 1949 were not so lucky. He had just finished junior school and had taken the 11+ exam as everybody did then. He was lucky in other ways too. His grandfather who was a builder had a splendid air-raid shelter that had kept Freddie and his older sister safe during the air raids and had made sure that his family didn't feel most of the hardships of the war. Freddie wasn't really aware of this. He had taken life for granted so far and it would be some years before he realised what a charmed life he had led.

So junior school was over. He had again taken this for granted, but the fact that he had enjoyed it meant that he had found the work was within his grasp pretty well all of the time. The teachers had been kind. The headteacher Mr Dean though a distant figure would periodically call Freddie to his office so that Freddie could read to him, all other pupils did the same. This was easy because Freddie had been taught to read by his Aunty Nell at a very early age during the war. Often she read to him in the Air-raid shelter when he was 5 or 6 years old.

Freddie learned early on that reading was fun, and his aunt made sure he had books he enjoyed. So going to junior school with a bunch of friends each day was a routine that he accepted as normal and he was happy.

When the results of the 11+ exam came through the letter box, Freddie's parents were delighted to find he had a place at the town grammar school. Freddie didn't really understand the implications, but he was pleased to see his parents were happy. During the August school holidays he was kitted out in the uniform worn only by the first years. This was a red blazer and red cap and grey flannel shorts. He learned later the first year was called the Remove. Why? No one ever told him. That year the family went to Devon for a holiday in his dad's canvas topped Morris Minor. It managed to get up the notorious Porlock Hill. Freddie didn't notice this because he was always car sick on any journey. The holiday was alright though and he enjoyed it. It was one of the first the family had had since the war other than going to the family caravan in Wales where he had been every school holiday for as long as he could remember.

Freddie's dad was away from 1939 till late in 1945. So, like so many of his friends he was 'dad-less' for most of his early years. When his dad came back it took some time to get used to. His dad, having been in the army, was used to orders, obedience and discipline. Freddie was the opposite, used to getting his own way and freedom. There was conflict of course and it took time for both of them to settle down. What Freddie learned in talking to friends, was that this was common to all of his mates whose dads had been in the forces.

Freddie and his sister moved back to their old house when his Granddad died in 1945. This house was backed by a railway line, single track only and though he was told it was important during the war for goods and war munitions which had to keep clear of the town and possible air-raids; now very few trains passed. This gave Freddie and his cousin Jim who lived next door, boundless possibilities of play on the embankment. Many adventures were had before he was ten. It wasn't just Jim, there was a gang, all boys from nearby houses. It was, of course, trespassing and a bicycle-riding policeman whom they knew often tried to catch them. Only once did he come close and they spent an hour cowering in their garage while he talked to Jim's dad. Nothing was said however and so play continued. In those days it was very different to now. Very few trains used the line and they could always hear them well before they appeared. Many things in those days would be frowned upon today, but life was easier then.

Most of the houses in the road were built at the same time before the war, mostly built by his Grandad's firm. So people moved in with similar ages, and thus they had children at similar times. So Freddie had a group of friends of his or Jim's age. Jim was 10 months older and that did put him in a class with older children. All the 'gang' walked to school together. No adults, not even when young. Surprising? I've said before, it was like that then. On Saturday mornings they would walk to the cinema, to the matinée, and watch exciting films with cowboys like Roy Rogers and his horse Trigger. This horse was clever and got him out of many scrapes. A favourite was Flash Gordon, a space adventurer. No one believed that space travel was possible of course, but Freddie loved it. On the way home the gang would act out an adventure of their own with either sticks for pistols or ray guns.

Boyhood was idyllic at this time. There were few clouds on any horizon. The war was over, peace was certain and rationing of sweets would surely end soon.

So Freddie went to the grammar school. It was not as easy as he expected, if he had expected anything. There was no one to tell him what to expect. Freddie just took it as it came. As you will see later there were unexpected problems for him which set him back seriously.

CHAPTER 2

After the summer holiday, secondary school loomed. Freddie was nervous. What would it be like? Would older boys bully him because he was not very big? Would he make friends? Freddie was very reliant on friends because he was not very outgoing and also not very confident till he knew people. Two or three of the boys from his class were due to go to the same school, but he thought, they might not be in the same class. So Freddie went to school on that first day feeling very nervous. It would have been useless had someone told him that almost every other boy in that first year was in the same boat. Freddie was an ordinary sort of boy and he was scared.

As it happened his panic did not last long. All new boys were ushered into the main hall, which he was told was called 'Big School'. Then lists were read out. He found he was to be in Remove A, the top set, the alpha stream. Alas, Dennis his best friend was in Remove B and then there was Remove C for anyone left. In his new form he had one friend Stewart who went trainspotting with him sometimes, but he didn't know anyone in Remove C.

Eventually the classes filed out to their classrooms. Freddie's was almost next door to the big hall. Like the hall it looked more like a church than a classroom, the windows were pointed like a church and there was some coloured glass in them. The boys had a desk each whereas in the junior school the desks were double, so Freddie always had a partner there. Also in the juniors all the desks were clean and new. Here was a surprising difference. The desk tops were carved with boys' initials some filled with ink. The lids of the desks lifted to reveal storage for books. The books were already in. They looked very old. The covers were again ink-stained and very often there were notes handwritten inside. For instance the Latin book called 'Latin Today' had an ink addition proclaiming it now to be 'Eatin Today'. Freddie thought this was funny, but then when he had time to look harder at the initials and dates carved on the desk, he realised many of the boys were long dead possibly during the First World War. He was getting an idea of just how old this school was.

The form teacher was called Mr Wilson and he did much to reassure Freddie that the school would not be too bad. At lunchtime, all boys ate in the same dining room. All stayed to dinner it appeared, at least in the lower years. Freddie found that Dennis did appear at this dinnertime, but was expected to go back the yard outside his separate building afterwards. This dismayed Freddie who felt the need for moral support among the crowd of older boys. However, he soon realised that these older and bigger boys had no interest in the first years and there was no bullying at all. Order in the playground, this was called the quad, was kept by prefects, many were 18 or even 19 years old. They seemed to have a great deal of power. They could give you lines to copy and even put you in detention after school. Nobody messed with prefects!

CHAPTER 3

"Finish your breakfast or you'll will be late again."

"Okay," Freddie said. He had been deep in thought throughout the meal. "Don't worry I shan't be late. I'm on my bike today and can be there in 20 minutes or so."

Freddie was very proud of the bike; he had had it for his 12th birthday. It was a Raleigh racer with dropped handlebars and four hub gears, very up-to-date and maroon red in colour. He thought it really stood out in the bike sheds at school. He had seen other boys looking possibly enviously at it. He finished dipping toast into his egg.

"Mum," he said, "I think my brain has woken up."

She looked at him hard. "What are you on about? You do come out with some strange ideas."

"Well," Freddie said, "I seem to have solved my algebra homework overnight. I'm going to have to write it out again in the school yard in the dinner hour 'cos I got it all wrong last night."

In Freddie's school, mathematics was divided into three separate subjects, taught in different lessons and sometimes by different teachers. Freddie liked geometry and coped with mathematics, but algebra was often a mystery.

His mother sighed, "You didn't have an easy start in that school. I wish your dad or I could have helped you. We didn't have your advantages, but we were so proud when you got your scholarship though. I'm sure you will do your best. Your last report left a lot to be desired you remember."

Freddie did remember and blushed slightly. He knew it wasn't entirely his fault. Freddie was still a smallish boy with mousey hair. He kept a low profile at school, but was not unpopular. He had a keen sense of humour and could make a joke out of anything, so he had always a small gang of friends in the quad. It was the meeting place whenever this group was freed from the perceived horrors of the classroom.

Freddie was now in his 3rd year at the local grammar school. The first year had been a succession of disasters. As he rode up the hill to the school, Freddie remembered the embarrassment of his first day. His first French lesson he had thought interesting. He had remembered to his astonishment that he had been put into the very top set, called the alpha Remove. He had found the 11+ exam that everyone took at this time hadn't been too taxing.

The school was the best in the town and he had been kitted out in the new boys' uniform. Freddie had been one of the smallest in his junior school class and had found it to be the same in the new school. His best friend Dennis, also small and skinny, had been put in the next class below. He thought Dennis wasn't very pleased with this, but as the months went by all was accepted. Dennis had been his best school friend since they were both six years old when Dennis had been transferred from another school that had presumably too many pupils. They had always been in the same class since that day when they had sat on the same dinner table.

 Freddie had eventually been told the school had existed since 1512. It felt like nothing very much had changed in the intervening years.

Freddie thought back to his first days in the school and remembered the books that had been through many hands and had tatty covers and notes in margins written by former students. It seemed that whatever was taught today had been taught for a good many years with little change. These books were now very familiar to him often going home in his satchel to be used for his homework.

Home time on that first day he had unpacked his satchel and did what he always did, tea, then out to play with lads in the road. He did go to bed a little earlier. Next day, more French was on his timetable. Freddie realised to his horror that he had forgotten that there was homework, only French on that first night but that was no consolation. He was supposed to have learned twelve French words. There was a test. Sir called out 12 English words one after the other. Freddie's paper was blank and even more embarrassing the paper was to be marked by the boy next to him. This was Stewart. He, Freddie, was the only boy to get zero. The class teacher Mr Wilson asked for the results in descending order and no other boy had less than eight correct. He had to explain himself and as a result Mr Wilson lectured the whole class on the privilege of being in the top form of a top school where all were expected to achieve O levels by the fourth year. He made it sound ominous as he glanced at a red-faced Freddie.

It was a lesson he was not likely to forget.

Mr Wilson was mainly an English teacher. One of the first

things he taught was a poem called 'Lake Island of Innisfree'. Freddie was not very big on poetry, but when Mr Wilson explained the poet W.B. Yeats was a personal friend, Freddie took more interest and memorised it. More importantly the teacher explained many poems could not be understood at their age, but if they committed them to heart, then they would make sense from time to time. Freddie always remembered these words, especially when later he was no longer in this class. Mr Wilson disappeared later that year. It was generally accepted he was ill, then later they heard that he had died. Freddie never learned the truth because no one spoke of it and boys like Freddie soon forgot. In these early days Freddie also had learned that whereas in the juniors he had teachers, now all teachers were called masters. All the masters were men, whereas in the junior school all teachers were ladies except for the Head and the woodwork teacher.

The French test was not the only disaster in his first year. In mid autumn term his father had said, "You aren't going to school today; we are going to get your nose dealt with."

Freddie didn't know anything was wrong with his nose, but his father had taken him to a doctor in the middle of the town who appeared to have a surgery in his house. It was all very disturbing. He was undressed, put in a gown. Very embarrassing. Then a sort of wicker mask was put on his face and a smelly liquid was dripped into the lint. Chloroform? Freddie neither knew nor cared. Count to ten he heard. When he woke later he was aware of a smell of burning. He felt sick. Later he learned that he had reacted very badly to cocaine that had been used as a pain control. He reacted so badly that the doctor and his father who had been allowed to watch the operation thought he might die. He'd had, he was told later, a fit of some sort. The actual operation wasn't too problematic, the cocaine had been. It meant a two-week convalescence. No school. The school had no system for making up lost time. He had returned to find things difficult. However, after the Christmas break he found himself escorted on the first day, from his form to Remove C which was in a separate older building some five hundred yards away from the main school. He left behind three friends who had come from the junior school. Worse was to come!

In the middle of the next term he was doing his Latin homework while his parents had made a very rare sortie to the local cinema. Freddie was worried, his anxiety grew, he was panicking. Would he ever get this right? His older sister Jean was upstairs, she was not able to understand his anxiety. Suddenly he started to cry in despair, he found he was unable to move. His sister came down and immediately went next door where his uncle and aunt lived. They had a telephone and phoned both the doctor and the cinema where his parents were about to have their evening spoiled. The upshot was that the doctor said he had experienced a sort of nervous breakdown and said he must take tablets of phenobarbitone to last for a month, and take another two weeks off school.

When he finally returned, Freddie wasn't sure whether his place in the school was safe. His report at the end of the year 1950 was dire. The Head had written, "He must look to his place in the school."

In the second year Freddie was in a class called Lower 3B. Dennis was in Lower 3A, but both were now in the main school dressed like everyone else in grey flannels, black jacket and a black cap with a red band. The year passed without any drama and Freddie survived the year though mostly in the lower ratings. His reports were definitely not good but not dire and the threat of losing his place seemed to have gone.

But, riding his bike up the hill to the school, he was now in the third year and a lot happier. He felt at home in the school and had attracted a small but pleasant group of friends. Dennis was of course always there in the breaks between lessons or the dinnertime. The schoolwork had grown harder, but he had some subjects where he coped but was never far from the lower end of the class. He actually enjoyed English as he was a great reader. He went to the local library and changed books weekly. Then in geography, he was a bit better, but maths, which was taught as three subjects, maths, algebra and geometry, well dismal might be used and Latin continued to haunt him.

This is how he went to school on that unusual day when he suddenly understood algebra. Freddie thought things were looking up, though why escaped him.

In the Maths class the homework was handed in and would be returned the following day. Freddie suddenly realised that neither he nor most of the class had ever got everything right. He would be accused of cheating, possibly having got an older boy to do the homework for him. How to explain that he could now see clearly how it all worked? He had one day to solve this. He could not say, "Sir, my brain woke up." Then he thought has it woken up in other subjects? He would worry about that tomorrow.

In the event the problem disappeared, Mr Allen, the Maths teacher, being a kindly man called Freddie out and put two algebra problems on the blackboard.

"Solve those, Windsor," he said.

Freddie walked out conscious that everyone was staring at him. The problems were harder than the homework and Freddie stared at the board, picked up the chalk and began to put the figures in. Each required three or four lines of figures and he grew in confidence.

"Well," said Sir, "you seem to have grasped the concept. Well done, sit down."

The class were suspiciously silent, Freddie was red faced and aware of glances in his direction. He daren't look anyone in the eye. Wasn't this the Windsor who was nearly always not far off the bottom of the class? What was going on? Freddie was aware he could lose friends. What to do? Mr Allen then went over Freddie's figures and this helped one or two of his friends who had found algebra difficult and this took attention away from him.

Music was held in a wooden hut some distance from the main school. Freddie trooped down to the building with a couple of friends. Canon Rust was the music teacher as well as RE as might be expected. He was playing a piece on the piano as they entered. He paused as the first boys came in. Before Freddie could help himself he said, "That was Liszt, wasn't it, Sir, one of his etudes?"

Canon Rust looked in amazement, "How do you know that, Windsor?"

"Er! My sister has a record player, Sir, and she likes classical music."

"And you have memorised it?" Canon Rust said.

"Well, I hear pieces every night while I'm doing homework."

Freddie was sweating. Would the lie hold up? He had no idea what possessed him to speak up or where the composer's name had come from. Who on earth was Liszt? This woken up brain was going to make life difficult if he didn't watch himself.

It was two days later when the 'Brain' got him into trouble again. So far, the incidents in Maths and music had been accepted by his friends as a symptom of his weirdness. They were all used to that.

Freddie's medical problem in the first year had been associated with Latin. Freddie could cope with the rather boring aspects, but could get little pleasure from the complex grammar. At the end of the next lesson, he found himself approaching the Doctor, as they called him.

"Sir, why is it we spend our time studying the stories of ancient Romans, Virgil and stuff, when Latin is used every day in science, such as the Linnean classification of all plants and animals? I collect cacti, Sir, and they all have a genus and species name in Latin and most species names are Latin adjectives. You have never mentioned this in class, Sir."

Freddie paused for breath. What had he said, what had he done?

The Doctor looked at Freddie with a bemused expression. Fortunately, all other boys had left.

"What has prompted this, Windsor? You are not renowned for Latin excellence, are you? Remind me what position in class were you last term?"

Freddie blushed, "I was pretty near the bottom, Sir."

"And now you are in position to criticise the school syllabus?"

"Er, no, Sir, I just thought."

"Well, take your 'just thought' away and turn in a decent homework and I might consider answering your question."

Scarlet-faced, Freddie left. This 'Brain' is a menace, it's out of control, he thought.

Later that day, a rather subdued Freddie sat down to tea. His dad had dinner much later when he got in from work. Freddie of course had a cooked dinner at school, so tea was a smaller meal.

"Mum, why can't we have spaghetti bolognese sometimes?" he said. "It's a very easy meal to make."

"What on earth is that," his mother said "and when have you ever had it?"

There was no obvious answer to this. Freddie not only had not had it, but he wasn't sure that he would like it. They had macaroni sometimes as a pudding and he wasn't keen on that. Oddly, Freddie thought he could see a plate of spaghetti in his mind and it looked delicious.

"You are coming out with some very strange things. I wonder if I should take your temperature."

"Er! I suppose I must have read about it," Freddie said, trying hard to end the conversation.

He quickly went to his room upstairs to do his homework. Tonight he had to write an essay on his hobby. Easy, he thought.

Freddie had been collecting cacti and succulent plants for a couple of years. They sat on a bench under his window that fortunately faced south, so giving them plenty of light. He had persuaded his mother to let him take the curtains down so they could have more light. He found cacti and succulent plants fascinating. He would spend his pocket money, which had just gone up to 5 shillings a week, at the local market where there was a stall selling them. The man was helpful, giving tips on how to look after them and propagate them. He liked Freddie and always let him have them slightly cheaper for being such a regular customer. Freddie would make up little bowls with mixed cacti and some rocks and sell them. This was mostly to his relatives. He was beginning to run out of relatives and was racking his brain to think how he might sell more in order to buy new stock of course. Cacti had become a sort of compulsion with him.

So, this essay was just up his street. Most boys in his class, he knew, would be writing about football and supporting the local team on Saturdays or stamp collecting or even train spotting as he used to do. He had a vague idea that his could be more interesting and he had learned quite a lot. He had a book on their care and had picked up extra knowledge from his friendly market stall chap. So, he worked till quite late. His mother knocked on his bedroom door before ten o'clock and suggested it was time for his light to go out.

"Shan't be long," he said, but it was nearly eleven o'clock when he finally put his pen down. He felt he had produced his best essay ever.

Freddie loved his new bedroom. Just as the 3rd year was beginning the family had moved to a brand new house his parents had had built by his uncle who was a builder. There had been a legacy from his Granddad that allowed them to do this. It had four bedrooms and only the two younger sisters had to share. Freddie's room was twice the size of his old one and had room for a desk as well as his growing cactus collection.

His Granddad had also left him half of a Hornby O gauge railway set. His cousin Jim had the other half and they had shared a transformer. Now Jim wasn't next door anymore, this was a problem and the train hardly ever came out of its box, even though he now had the space to lay it out. Freddie thought of it sometimes; perhaps one day he would be able to buy a replacement transformer and perhaps some extra rails, but these were all very expensive items.

The essays were handed in next day to his form teacher, 'Dickie Dance'. This teacher he really liked, he had humour and was never played up even by the 3rd years. All teachers knew that 3rd years were generally known to be a very difficult lot. Mr Dance taught English and History. These subjects were Freddie's best, even though his last report had read 'Windsor finds Shakespeare difficult.' Freddie knew that this wasn't true; he actually enjoyed it as with all books. He had been near the bottom of the class in that term. Perhaps Mr Dance had confused him with someone else, he thought. Anyway this would show him. It would, but not quite as Freddie expected.

Two days later English class started and the essays were handed out. Freddie saw immediately that instead of a number score it just had the word 'excellent' in blue ink on the top.

All the boys contemplated the comments they had earned.

"Windsor," he heard, "bring your essay to the front of the class!"

He went scarlet as he usually did when the centre of attention and sheepishly stood in front of his friends and classmates.

"Windsor has a rather unusual hobby," he heard Mr Dance say. There was a slight snigger from the far corner of the room where a trio of the more disreputable pupils sat. He tried to ignore it; he was embarrassed enough already. "Read on," said 'Dickie Dance'.

"All vegetative plants will at sometimes in their lives flower, set seed and so reproduce themselves, but with cacti this may take many years for they live in a very hostile environment. This is not, however, their most surprising secret."

Mr Dance stopped him. "Did you get that sentence out of a book, Windsor?" He said it kindly, not accusingly.

"No, Sir," Freddie said. "I just know this about them."

"Well, it's that sentence that brought you out to front, so carry on, tell us more."

The rest of the essay explained the well-known facts, well known to Freddie but probably no one else in his class or school. He explained that all cacti were succulents but not all succulents were cacti. He explained in the essay that cacti were unique to the Americas, that they had spines which were modified leaves and though there were spiky succulents in Africa and even southern Europe, spines were unique to true cactus. He explained how the plants stored water, could go for long periods without any and had different ways of doing this. Succulents grew in all the major continents; in the Americas they were often spiky but never had true spines.

He mentioned one of his favourite succulents Sempervivum arachnoides. This, he said, had baby plants growing out from it which could be harvested and grown on. It was Freddie's favourite because he could get an endless supply for his little cactus bowls which added to his pocket money. He explained the Latin. "The species," he said, "means spider-like and the genus means ever living, because of this constant supply of baby plants. The plants are very hairy, a defence against the sun; I have seven of them."

The class erupted. They had been very good listeners so far, but for Freddie to admit he had seven hairs brought out the worst in them. They were 14 year olds after all.

Freddie's talk had ended, but he had got into his stride and was feeling pleased with himself despite the laughing and some boys noted Mr Dance had also joined in.

"Stay there, Freddie," he said "Has anyone any questions?"

His friend John's hand shot up. "How do you know all this and how come you're suddenly teaching us Latin?"

It's a good job you're a friend, thought Freddie. "I read books and all plant names are in Latin, also animal names," he added. This was an afterthought.

The next question was harder, but Freddie came out with answers that he didn't actually know, and question followed question, each harder. Freddie answered them all with a smooth flow and a smile on his face. It was the 'Brain' again taking him over completely. He explained that cacti had evolved in South America and had only moved into North America when the isthmus of Panama had made a land bridge 5 million years ago. That cacti had probably only had 10 million years of evolution, though this was uncertain because unlike some other things fossils could neither form nor be found. He went on to explain the uniqueness of the arioles which were the true diagnostic of a cactus, how their original leaves which lost water gradually shrank into hard spines which of course protected them from grazing herbivores. He had to explain some of his terms. He remembered that they had not mentioned an isthmus in geography yet.

Freddie stopped. The questions ran out and his answers had lasted the whole of the lesson. He was aware everyone was staring at him. Oh drat! he thought, I've blown it now.

Mr Dance said, "Thank you, Freddie, and thank you for those who supplied some interesting questions to which Freddie seems to have given some remarkable answers. That was enlightening."

Freddie understood that there were two ways to take that comment! But he had never been called Freddie by a teacher before and he suspected it had been noticed by the class.

"Well, sit down, though I think we can all pack away; the bell will go any minute."

It did and Freddie had to face his friends.

Outside of the classroom there was a small gathering only, to his relief. There were the usual three trouble makers with smug looks on their faces. There was Billy Helme and Brian Bennett, Terry and Bunny and a couple of others. Lucky for him his best friend Dennis turned up from his own class at that moment.

"What's up?" said Dennis.

"Your mate has only taken over a whole English lesson and Dickie let him," said one of the three. "He was talking about cacti for 40 minutes."

"Oh," Dennis said, "he knows a lot about them."

The three slouched off bored.

"Hang on," said Billy, "this wasn't just about cacti. He was talking about stuff I didn't understand and I don't think Dickie understood either, I was watching his face. He was boggling. In fact, I don't think I'm his favourite anymore. Your mate is. Well, it's a relief to me, good luck to you, Freddie, enjoy it, but watch yourself."

At this Billy, John and Terry left.

"What's going on?" said Dennis.

"Er nothing really," Freddie said. "I read my essay, which I thought was rather good and Dickie asked if anyone had questions. They did and it went on a bit."

"Could you answer them?"

"Yes, in fact but I'm not sure how all the answers came into my mind."

"I expect you read it all sometime," Dennis said.

"Yes, I expect you're right," said Freddie, feeling very relieved that he had got away with it yet again.

John - I had asked Freddie the first question in the English class. Freddie had easily confused me with his answer, but I recognised he knew what he was talking about. I had sat next to Freddie in Art for most our time in the school. He got on well with me and Mike who sat on the other side of him. He had always been very quiet and I didn't find him very interesting I admit. This was a new Freddie. He was so confident, I was rather jealous. How could this boy speak with so much knowledge and to the whole class without a break in the flow of stuff. I didn't understand much of what he was saying. He appeared to be speaking a new language. OK, he chucked Latin phrases in regularly. He went on for whole lesson and whatever anyone asked him he knew the answer. Weird!

Billy - I was always the one to read the main part in whatever Shakespeare play we were reading. There is no doubt Dickie liked me. On one occasion he had asked if anyone who had a bike would cycle to his house to pick up some books he had left at home. I noticed that Freddie offered and I knew he lived near Dickie, but he chose me rather than Freddie. I went. It was about 20 minutes by fast bike. A large brown house close to a canal. The lady who answered the door was elderly; I assumed his mother rather than his wife. She said she could not climb the stairs to his rooms and I would have to go up alone. I did and found his room filled with books and papers and stuff about the Greeks and Romans. I found on his desk the books he had told me about and took them down the stairs. The lady asked me if I would like some tea or cake, but I told her the books were needed urgently, so quickly back to school. But now I realised that Freddie had replaced me as number one pupil in our class. I didn't mind, you can have too much attention sometimes and it can be embarrassing.

Freddie - That night, Freddie in bed thought back to the incidents that had occurred since 'his brain woke up'. Okay, he had some awkward moments, but on the plus side he had earned a bit of respect from maths, English and music and possibly a bit of respect from people like Billy and John whom he rather admired for their confidence and the fact they seemed to know far more about life generally than he did. However, the disturbing thought came that 'the brain' was feeding him stuff he really didn't know. All that cactus stuff, he knew he hadn't read it. Dennis as usual had got him off the hook. Should he let Dennis into his secret? No answer. He turned over and tried to sleep. Sleep would not come and his mind kept coming back to the same question. What was this 'brain stuff'? Where did the stuff that came into his mind come from? Was it his own thoughts or were the thoughts from outside of himself? This last idea was deeply disturbing, but there were no answers from his 'Brain' when he would have welcomed them. Eventually, he slept.

Next day, his 'English lesson' had faded from most people's memory. But Billy came up to him and said, "Hello, smartarse, I suppose you will come top in English this term."

He said it a friendly way and Freddie blushed. Billy didn't usually speak to him at all. Others smiled at him as he went into class. He had gained some friends he thought. Well done 'Brain'.

Music again this week and he was very cautious going in and there were several in the room already. Canon Rust looked up from the piano. He was not playing anything to Freddie's relief.

"Hello, Windsor", he said, "I thought I would test your repertoire" and with that he turned to the piano and began a virtuoso performance, his hands moving up and down the keys with speed and the sound was beautiful. He really was very good. It came to an end and he grinned and looked at Freddie. "Well! what did you make of that?"

Freddie didn't really think, he just answered. "Well Sir, it has all the hallmarks of Beethoven, he really is unmistakable. He wrote an awful lot of pieces, so I'm not sure if this is a fair test. But if I have to opt for one I would say his 5th piano concerto, the Emperor, maybe. That's one of my favourites."

There was a stunned silence from the class, most of whom had now arrived and heard Freddie's answer. They of course thought he was showing off and guessing. However, the Canon's mouth was agape.

"Astonishing," he said. "Surely your sister's collection is not this advanced?"

"Ah no," said Freddie, "but my friend's father, who lives opposite, has a large collection and I like Mozart and Beethoven especially." The 'Brain' had supplied him with this lie and the escape in the nick of time.

"Well," said the Canon, "we will see how far your musical abilities go. Do you play an instrument, Freddie?"

There it was! Yet another teacher was using his first name. Freddie felt a warm glow. Well done 'Brain', he thought.

"No, Sir, I don't. We have a piano at home and my younger sister Diana has piano lessons, but my mum thought piano lessons would get in the way of homework when I was 11. I did find the first year very hard, Sir."

Canon Rust knew Freddie's school history and said no more. "Right sit down, lad." Privately he wondered if he had missed a chance of developing this lad in his first year. Perhaps he could have introduced him to an instrument? He clearly loved music.

In the grammar school 3rd year, the pupils had had to choose to do either science, chemistry and physics. There was no biology in the school, it was far too new a science, or they could choose art and geography. General science had been promised, but this had mysteriously disappeared after one term. Freddie was left with confusion as a result, for instance, about how electricity worked. He'd had an analogy of water flowing through pipes with taps instead of switches. It didn't make sense, but they never got to the point where it would make sense. Dennis had chosen both sciences. What this meant in real terms was that for some of the lessons boys from both the B and C streams were mixed up depending on their choices. The streams had always been together for games. Freddie liked this because he had a greater choice of potential and actual friends even though he mostly saw Dennis only at break times.

Games was a rather strange affair. Two periods on one afternoon but by the time they were changed at both ends, it was less than an hour. In the summer, cricket or preparations for sports day and in winter always football. The two classes together had more boys than the teams that were picked. Small boys like Freddie and Dennis and others were hardly ever picked. The team captains wanted to win after all. So, they were given a ball to kick and left to their own devices. The other boys called this bunch the 'Stragglers'. Not very flattering but it had always been so as far back as anyone could remember, like so much else in this strange old-fashioned school. Once in a while the games and PE teacher would suggest a cross-country run and they would run round the block. Freddie liked this; he was a fast runner having spent most of his life with access to an old railway embankment, and in his new house this and a canal towpath. He tended to run more than he walked. In PE Freddie was much better. Right from the start his skinny body and light weight meant he could easily climb a rope, vault the horse and box apparatus and pull himself easily up and over the beams. He was not so good at handstands. Against the wall bars was OK, but freestanding he always overbalanced. Still, it did mean he really enjoyed gym lessons and the PE master did take more notice of him.

In the third year, he had opted for art and geography because he had always held his own in these subjects and in art he had perhaps the nicest teacher in the school. This was Mr Viner. The art class was like a haven of peace. Mr Viner never raised his voice and his criticisms were always positive. In art, Freddie sat between Brian Bennett and another of his best friends, Michael Warren. Mike was a keen bird watcher. He spent all his weekends at local lakes, sewage farms and anywhere else something unusual might turn up. He kept sketchbooks filled with his drawings, many of which were not complete birds but parts of them and in some cases the bushes, trees and locations of the birds. These were very good and Freddie felt quite privileged to have been shown them. In every topic 'Charlie Viner' gave to them 'Willy' Warren put in a bird. Freddie of course put in a cactus. It says a lot about their teacher that he indulged their little ways.

On this particular day the topic was different. Mr Viner decided to introduce them to some of the 'Old Masters'. He had a projector device and a screen set up in front. The art class was in a large room with windows on two sides and there were only about 20 boys in the class. They gathered close to the screen. The size of the pictures was not great. It was lucky that the weather was gloomy and it was last lesson in early spring. Light was fading.

The first picture was a picture of flowers in orange with a darker centre. "What do any of you think of this picture?" said Charlie.

Brian Bennett's hand went up. "Well, Bennett?"

"Flowers," said Brian.

"Well!" said Mr Viner, "a quite remarkable observation, Bennett!"

Brian reddened.

"Anyone else?"

Freddie felt himself getting to his feet.

"Sir, I think it is what can be described as a Dutch Old Master. I guess it may be by Vincent Van Gogh, perhaps the greatest of them all."

'Well done, Windsor," said Charlie. "Might I enquire how you gained this insight?"

Here we go again, thought Freddie. "Well, Sir, I read an awful lot and I suppose I came across it."

"Good," said Charlie and moved on to the next. "You are quite correct in your guess."

The next picture was of a man sitting on a beach and a girl or boy balancing on a ball. There was a lot of blue in the painting.

"Well?" said Charlie. "Thoughts?"

No one spoke. No one wanted the embarrassment Brian had had. Freddie again felt a stirring inside his head. Oh no, he thought, stop, please stop. 'Brain' would not.

"It's a Picasso from his blue period and I think it is called 'Girl on a Ball', for obvious reasons, though you can't really tell whether it's a boy or girl".

"Well, well!" said his teacher, "very good, and can you tell us what else this famous artist painted?"

Freddie hesitated. He wished he didn't have an answer, but unfortunately 'Brain' did.

"Well, Sir, I should think the disturbing picture called Guernica is his best known for rather sad reasons."

"Windsor, tell us about the picture and why does that particular picture make you feel sad?"

He could now see a very clear picture of the Guernica masterpiece in his mind.

"It's a strange mixture of disfigured people and weird animals; they are only partly drawn but some have their hands in the air as if they feel things falling on them. I believe it has its origins in the Spanish civil war and the horrors of early bombing of towns, perhaps looking to what would happen in our times. I experienced bombing in Bristol during the war when I was young, Sir, so I feel this picture speaks to me."

Freddie sat down. He had tears in his eyes and Mr Viner could see them.

"Thank you, Freddie. You have expressed exactly what I

was hoping for by showing these famous pictures. I think the lesson has been very successful thanks to your insights."

At the end of the lesson, Mr Viner said, "Windsor, um, Freddie, could you hang back for a minute. Freddie, I am not going to ask how you know so much. I have been talking to Mr Dance. It appears you have been 'hiding your lights under a bushel' since the first year. What I would like to know is why at your age you can express so much emotion for a painting. But I am so glad you did not attempt to hide it as most boys of your age would."

Freddie thought. Would 'Brain help'? Here goes, he thought, let 'Brain' have its way.

"Well, Sir," his usual opening when trying to buy time, but it wasn't really necessary this time. "The picture moved me. The strangeness of the images, I saw fear in it and destruction and who would not be moved by that. I was scared in Bristol when I was only 6 or so. A bomb fell so close to us, we were in a cellar in a stone house near the suspension bridge and we felt the house shake and heard the noise."

Freddie had in fact only ever known war from his earliest memories. For most of his young life till he was 7½, he spent most nights in air raid shelters wearing a siren suit. He heard the wailing of sirens both the warning and the all clear. At the bottom of his Granddad's garden where the air raid shelter was, there was a barrage balloon to protect an ack ack gun. This rarely fired, but the balloon helped protect the shelter as well. No enemy airplane would dare fly low and risk destruction. Even when he went to the junior school, regular drills were carried out and they would all troop to the large school shelters.

Charlie smiled kindly at him.

"Well done, Freddie, off you go. You impressed me today, you are an unusual boy."

Freddie left. What on earth would happen next? Teachers were beginning to talk. Word was getting around. Should he have a word with Dennis. Would Dennis think he was bonkers?

For a couple of weeks nothing unusual happened. Teachers who had experienced his 'outbursts' left him alone, but carried on using his name. This was very unusual in the school where surnames only were used. True a teacher might pick up a boy's nickname and use it if it was amusing. It did mark Freddie out a bit, but it got to be accepted in class.

One unusual thing occurred soon after. Two or three of them used to go in the lunch hour to a nearby place that both manufactured Vimto in little bottles and sold crisps. Each of these cost 2 pence. It was rare everybody had all the coins they needed. On this occasion Terry was with them.

"I only have a threepenny bit and a halfpenny," said Terry.

"I will lend you a halfpenny," said Dennis and he got out his small purse with a flap on it and extracted the coin. The boys used to laugh at Dennis's purse, except when they needed a loan. "But you must pay me back a penny tomorrow."

"Hang on," said Freddie, "that is 100% interest per day!"

"Well," said Dennis, "take it or leave it."

Terry took it. 'Brain' kicked in.

"You will be an accountant when you leave school," Freddie said.

"Some chance," said Dennis. But Freddie knew it would happen. He had a picture of Dennis as an adult in his mind. How could he know the future? More importantly, he knew they would still be friends. This was scary. Dennis seemed to forget this forecast fortunately.

In February of that year, all boys were suddenly summoned to the large school hall, a very ancient building much like a church, filled with plaques showing old boys' scholarships and lists of those who had been killed in the two World Wars. The teachers were all there looking solemn. The Head strode up the aisle looking only at the floor ahead. On the platform he turned and said, "The King is dead, long live the Queen. You will all go home now the school is closed till tomorrow."

The news was so shocking, there had been no warning. There was none of the usual hub-bub or chatter. All trooped out and went home where Freddie found that on the wireless both the Home Service and the Light Programme were playing only solemn music. It was very strange, almost as if the world had stopped. Freddie was sad, King George had been his King all his life and he remembered his courage during the War. All this knowledge had been gained from newsreels at Saturday cinema.

Another week passed without incident, and Freddie was travelling home on the bus. His bike had a puncture and his dad usually fixed it for him. He had time to think both on the bus ride and on the walk home.

This school is very odd, he thought. I've been in it three years and yet it isn't like any other school around here. No one else I know has as much homework or is pushed as hard as we are.

He thought back to his short time in the alpha stream. In fact, he hardly ever saw those boys he had left behind. They worked even harder and disappeared rapidly to do their homework, music lessons and so on. Freddie felt very relieved to be where he was. Those boys were going to do O levels in English language and English literature and maths at the end of the next year. This would give them time to concentrate on their Latin and Greek as well as French, which all boys took. Most even added an extra language. What on earth for? A prefect had explained to him that most of the 'alphas' had their eyes set on famous universities and would then go on to careers in the civil service, law and government generally. Freddie couldn't understand how Latin and Greek came into this.

Freddie felt he had had a narrow escape. He did not want a career like that. Not that he knew what he did want. The 'Brain' seemed to have given him an uncanny knowledge of music, but what good was that? He realised that everything he had been told in these amazing outbursts had stayed in his head. In fact, not only had he forgotten nothing, but he seemed to have had loads of extra knowledge put in as well. What good was all this musical knowledge going to do him? Not that he didn't enjoy it, he did. 'Brain' had expanded his repertoire. He was now listening to Baroque composers in his head, Handel, Scarlatti, Vivaldi and especially Bach. Music was in his head a lot of the time when he was on his own. But what good would it do him? But he did love listening to Bach.

In the last week of term, the last 3rd year reports were given out. He was, as he and the rest of the class expected, top of the class in English. Wasn't he now Mr Dance's favourite pupil? He stayed top for the rest of his school career and was careful not to be top in too many other subjects. True he was close to top in many things, but just low enough not to attract too much attention.

His improvement was largely due to his ability to cross-question his brain without his being taken over by it. He treated it like the Encyclopaedia Britannica that his uncle, who, when they were in their old house, lived next door and had been collecting the 26 volumes over many months. If he asked, he generally got an answer. Or perhaps he imagined it all and he was paying more attention, but he knew this was not true. Over these many weeks he was no nearer to understanding where his knowledge came from.

Anthony Winnall

CHAPTER 4

A new year, a new class, a new form teacher and by now the differences in the two classes was invisible. They were mixed up for so many things. Freddie liked this. More friends together pretty well all day. Also now he was approaching 15, friends were meeting more out of school. They would cycle to each other's houses or meet up at the cinema or the town baths. Freddie 'the ordinary sort of boy' was happy.

"Hello, I'm Freddie."

So far someone else has been describing my life, as if looking over my shoulder. I've always felt someone was! But now I'm talking to you directly, because I want to tell you not only what happened, but what I thought and felt and no outsider can do that, can they? Perhaps not all of my thoughts and feelings, somethings do need to be a bit private, don't they? I'm sure you know what I mean. I hope you will stay with my strange story even if you're thinking, "This boy is strange, or worse!" Well, I can accept that, it's only what my friends think, or at least I think it is. Since the events were strung out over a year and more, there was time between each incident for them to lose interest and generally forget. Okay my place in form had improved beyond belief. It could have gone further, but I held 'Brain', as I call it, in check as far as I could and cunningly made the odd deliberate mistakes both in class and in homework, in order not to get perfect scores. In English I didn't need to do this. It was accepted that I read an awful lot and Billy Helme didn't mind me displacing him. In fact, we became quite friendly, not that he joined my little gathering near the bike sheds. Oh no! he was much too superior for that or more likely he was developing interests we had not yet developed. I think it was probably girls.

In the other subjects, teacher's comment about being "a late developer" was accepted both by the teachers and by my classmates. I thought, 'instant developer' might have been truer, but I never said this, of course.

I was living a strange life. Schoolwork had become rather easy and I still had all my friends. It was beginning to become obvious that I was feeling the need to know more and more. I could not be bored and I felt this inside my head, not school work but much wider. If I accidently got ahead of the syllabus, someone would 'smell a rat'. I must be careful. Better to start something the school didn't cover. I made one exception. The music! I recognised that the Canon's class was actually interesting me and I thought, he won't mind if I know a 'little' more will he?

My sister Jean, who is four years older, had left school and was often out in the evenings now. This gave me opportunities because I took over her record player and radio. So 'Brain' could now reveal great parts of Mozart's repertoire. I could see in my head both orchestral, choral and solo works. I loved them. I also learned about his life. In order to cover this, I had dropped in to Uncle's in order to consult the Encyclopaedia, but now after the move this was not so easy. Anyway, I had never discovered anything that I was already being told, but it used to be good cover. An opportunity to reveal a tiny part of 'my new interest' came quite soon. I hadn't stopped to consider why I was doing this 'reveal'. I was sure I could get away with it. Was I starting to show off? That would be a slippery slope. No, I had this fixed idea and 'Brain' didn't warn me or put the brakes on.

Jean - Freddie has always been a bit of a pain since he was quite small. During the war I noticed he was always taken by Mum to the places where my dad was stationed. Sometimes I was left with Nanny and Grandad. I was, I think, a little jealous of this, though rationally he was four years younger and I suppose Mum felt he had to be taken. I suppose I should have been proud to be considered able to be left, but it didn't always feel like that. When we were older and I was playing with my friends, sometimes he and Jim would turn up and spoil things. So was I desperately keen on my younger brother? No! Then he suddenly changed. He wanted my record player, a Dansette which I had bought with pocket money. Then he wanted my radio. I gave way in the end because he was persistent. I had no idea what all this was about, but then since I had left school I was finding more interesting things to do. I do think my younger brother is a little weird though.

Freddie - We only had one lesson of music a week, probably because for us it wasn't an exam subject, just a timetable filler I suppose. As my friends and I walked into the music room, Canon Rust saw me and he smiled and started to play Mozart. I could see that he wanted to tease me a little. I didn't sit down, but moved nearer to the piano. He looked up and smiled again; he could see I had accepted the challenge. The piece ended and he said, "Well, Freddie?"

I tried to appear thoughtful, though I was almost bursting with inner laughter.

"Well," I said, as solemnly as I could manage and avoiding any smile. "Mozart wrote so much I must have a moment or two." It was hard to keep a straight face. "I think you have set a trap for me and I think you will expect me name a piano concerto, but it isn't. It isn't a concerto at all. It was written for a full orchestra, and what you have transposed for the piano is the very well known opening of Symphony No. 35, generally known as the Haffner. It's one of my favourite symphonies, there is so much life in it. I find it uplifting, however it lacks the complexity of No. 41, the Jupiter, which I think is the best he wrote."

The Canon grinned broadly. "Yes, Freddie, it was a test or 'trap' if you must call it that, but I was assuming it was well known enough for you to stand a chance. Tell me how do you know it so well and what else do you know about the Jupiter?"

I was ready for this, and didn't need any 'inside my head' help. "My sister has given me her record player and I bought the Haffner LP." Not entirely a lie, the record player was now in my bedroom, but not yet strictly mine.

"And about the Jupiter?" he said.

"Well, Sir," I said, "it was his last and he probably died without hearing it performed. Its complexity somehow links back to Baroque, I think. Anyway, its very different," I added rather lamely.

"Remarkable," he said. He was silent for a moment and then he said, "Sit down." I did. He suddenly had a thought.

"Freddie, how did you know the word transposed? You don't, regrettably, do music as one of your choices."

I was for a moment or two perplexed. I hadn't expected this. Was this punishment by 'Brain' for being so cocky? I was silent for a while and oddly on this occasion nothing came into my head. I read it, Sir, wasn't going to wash.

"I'm not sure, Sir."

That actually was the best answer I could have given because it gave the Canon a chance to explain what he had done to the rest of the class and he gave several more examples and attention moved away from me. It made an interesting class. I sat down and breathed a sigh of relief.

At the end of the lesson Canon Rust said, "Freddie, would you mind remaining behind for a moment."

I felt panic. Was I going to mess up the whole thing? I stood by the piano and he smiled up at me; I relaxed.

"What do you know about Mozart himself?" he asked me.

I thought, this might be tricky, take care. I told him some of the basic facts that I thought most grown-ups would know and which I might easily have come across. How he had been a child prodigy and been taken round the European Courts. I said I 'thought' he had written more than 40 symphonies; I knew the real number. I said he wrote concertos for piano, clarinet, in fact for almost every instrument. I expressed sorrow that he had died at 35, so young with his Requiem not quite finished and had been buried in a pauper's grave despite the many commissions he had received. I had deliberately not given the actual numbers of the different compositions.

No one is that clever, are they? He seemed thoughtful and dismissed me.

The Canon - I had the most extraordinary incident in class today. A boy whom I had hardly noticed, in a class which is not doing Music for O level, has displayed some unusual knowledge. It had taken me by surprise. For the most part this class was a problem. They were my timetable filler. They for the most part showed no great interest in the subject. I remembered that this boy, Windsor, I think he was called, had occasionally been able to identify fairly quickly any piece that I had played. It hadn't particularly registered with me, but now he was coming out with the most amazing knowledge for a fourteen-year-old. In one lesson he had identified a Liszt etude, and in the next a Beethoven concerto. What fourteen-year-old knows about Liszt, let alone what an etude is? I must explore just how much he does know.

Freddie - Had I learned a lesson? Er no! Every time I got away with something there was an inner urge to try something else. I was getting reckless. However, nothing dramatic happened during the rest of the term and the summer holidays arrived.

I was at the seaside bay where we had our holiday caravan as usual and was far too busy enjoying myself to be thinking of school work or anything else which may have stretched my mind. We stayed in the family caravan which had been there for a long time. There had been only five caravans in the bay for years, but recently two of my uncles had added theirs, but other families stayed in tents. My cousins were almost always there for extended stays, as were several of my friends who lived near my old house, in all a fun gang of us, with long days spent on the beaches and cliffs. We knew about tides and were in no danger of being cut off. In any case we also knew where there were parts of the cliff which were climbable.

So, I was now in the fourth year and would be 15 half way through. My birthday is in March so I was exactly average for the class. Bunny was older, birthday in January and Dennis was as young as anyone was likely to be with a birthday in July, but then we found Mike Warren was actually a full year behind having entered the school at 10, clever chap. We didn't tease him; he was too inoffensive and he was certainly able to hold his own.

The next incident came out of the blue and suggested that though I had been relaxing, 'Brain' had not. Was it 'Brain' which wanted to be centre of attention, not me? It was so different from anything so far that I could not have anticipated it. I found it so unreal that I couldn't have dreamt it either.

It happened in the autumn term. I had been coasting along ensuring I kept my marks just under perfect as teachers had learned to expect and I had become rather blasé. There were no challenges in the lessons and I had little reason to challenge 'Brain' very often. Perhaps 'Brain' was getting bored with me and wanted to show another side of "its", "his" self? If it was, I was rather hoping it might reveal insight and or knowledge in a subject that might show an opening to a career. After all, next year I would be taking O levels and almost certainly leaving school. I certainly didn't want to stay alongside the linguists with their carefully planned and, I believed, extremely boring futures. It would be handy if it were to be something the school didn't do, then I could relax and I would not need to reveal it in school. I hoped it would not involve knowing the future because that could be very dangerous and it would get me labelled a freak. No one would believe my foreknowledge could come true, not for years anyway. By then they would have forgotten I had predicted it. In the end both of these things happened.

We were gathered in the schoolyard in the dinner hour, having survived a meal of the two of my least-liked meals. The dinner was liver. I always had to force this down and the pudding was sago. Slimy frogspawn we called that.

I should remind you, that though the war finished in 1945 and it was now spring 1952, times were still difficult. Many things were still rationed, meat especially; in fact, we seemed to live mostly on corned beef imported from Argentina. Luckily, I liked this in the many different forms it turned up and we had it at home as well. The worst thing affecting all the kids I knew was that sweets had stayed on ration though some things like flour had come off. Sweets did come off ration in 1949 but only for two months or so. There had been such a rush people bought whole jars at a time if they could afford it, so rationing started up again. At least it was raised to where we were on that day, 4ozs a week or one Mars bar.

We were discussing the rather disgusting school dinner, a combination of two horrid foods in everybody's opinion. The talk turned to sweets. We all remembered the chaos of 1949.

I said, "Never mind, on the 4th of February in 1953 it will end and we can have whatever our pocket money will buy." This date was not very far off.

There was silence, they were all looking at me.

"Blimey! You can't possibly know that. You may be right on the year, but you can't know the date. How can you claim to know it?" someone said.

"What are you, a prophet or something?" someone else said.

I didn't know what to say. I read it somewhere, wouldn't wash. Oh! A lucky guess wouldn't either. It just came to me, would raise suspicion and might make them remember some of my other oddities. I knew no one who might have a link to government's thoughts. 'Brain' was silent. I felt my face colouring. They were looking at me accusingly.

"I sometimes have these thoughts," I said lamely.

A few accepted this, many didn't. Dennis gave me a very hard look. I could see he was going to question me in private later. Someone changed the subject.

"Tod Owen is giving a test tomorrow."

He was the Geography teacher. Before I could stop myself, I said, "Don't worry, he will be off sick tomorrow and for three days so you'll have plenty of time."

Doom! Not only would they be able to test my 'prophecy', but they would see how accurate it was and it was something I could not possibly know. I dreaded tomorrow. I still had no logical answers for them.

Of course, it happened and new young teacher came in. He took up where Mr Owen had left off and though we viewed him very carefully, he was generally treated with respect. No one played up in geography. The lesson ended and we spilled out into the school yard. The usual crowd was waiting.

"Okay," they said, "how did you know?"

Dennis had given me a lukewarm answer. "Oh! I expect I heard two teachers saying he wasn't well."

"That's all very well," one said. "You gave an exact time he would be off."

This was very accusing.

"Oh!" I said, "must have been a guess."

It didn't convince many, especially Dennis, who had the night before demanded to know what was going on. That would have to wait till the weekend. When Mr Owen returned exactly as 'prophesied', I would have some more explaining to do because the mythical teachers could not have known that either. Coincidence would not wash.

Worse was to come, Terry had been in the group who had heard the 'prophecy' and when I saw him the following day, I approached him and said, and I could not stop myself saying it, "Terry, you are going to spend most of your life very far away, possibly at the other end of the world, but when you are old you and I will be talking to each other."

I had absolutely no idea how this came to me or how we could be talking. He looked at me blankly and said, "Yes, yes, yes, and I am the Queen of Sheba!"

I understood from this comment that he had more than a certain amount of scepticism. I left it there.

Terry - When Freddie told me I would spend my life at the other end of the World, my first thought was, Please, not Antarctica, I don't like the cold. Then I thought, Don't be daft, Freddie, I'm going to try the 6th form. Then I remembered my dad had talked about a scheme where you could go to Australia or New Zealand for ten pounds. I didn't think he was serious, but it gave me food for thought. Some of Freddie's strange predictions had come true. I put it out of my mind. Exams were coming, that was enough to think about.

Bunny - I was there when Freddie came out with the most extraordinary stuff about a teacher being away for a few days. It seemed extraordinary that he should have the nerve to say it. But he said it with such confidence as if he was in full knowledge of a teacher's illness. It wasn't possible, of course. He knew that, I knew that and yet he persisted. Was he a nutter? Well, I had known Freddie for three years and I thought he had weird episodes. I didn't think he was deranged. Of course, when we found out he was correct in his "prophecy", I was bewildered. Was this the same boy I had known since he appeared in our class in the second term of our first year? I have to admit I was confused.

Freddie - That weekend I met with Dennis and we had a heart to heart. I told how suddenly all this had come on me and how many times I had opened my mouth I had no idea what would come out. I didn't tell him of the things 'Brain' had been filling my mind with that did not clash with schoolwork, the music and so on. He knew I had suddenly progressed in my class and had put it down to the fact that I had originally been placed in the top stream for a term. I swore him to secrecy, but he did say that he could not keep finding excuses for me. I trusted him because we had been such close friends for so long, but it was obvious that in many ways I was now on my own.

I have mentioned we had moved to a new house. It had been built on a field that was quite overgrown. My dad had worked hard at weekends building small walls because the land sloped down to a brook, which at times was a small river. He had laid lawns and I had helped him put a pond into the back garden. On this day, he had asked if I would like help plant a large flower bed in the front garden. I was, as you know, keen on plants and we planted up lupins and delphiniums. Dad had grown these from seeds of earlier plants and it would be fun to see how many different colours we could get. But I found that this was not why he had asked my help.

"Your mum and I are worried about you, Freddie," he said somewhat awkwardly.

"In what way, Dad?" I said.

"Well," he said slowly, "you are doing better at school, your last report was better than we could possibly expect. The improvement seems to have been remarkably fast. You seem to have taken up a lot of new interests, music for instance, you are always listening to Jean's record player and buying or borrowing records of pretty highbrow music, yet it's not a subject you're taking an exam in."

I remained silent to see what else he would say.

"Your mother says she sees that sometimes you seem very worried despite your homework being easier. She picks this up very easily; she remembers what happened when you were younger. I worry that you tell me you want to leave school at the end of your fifth year. What do you want to do, Freddie? Have you any ideas?"

It was a lot to answer and I wanted to be as honest as possible.

"I'm not sure, Dad, but I have been giving it a lot of thought. It's clear to me that the sixth form in my school would be very limiting. I haven't been doing the subjects they normally cover in the sixth and those things have never really interested me.

I would like to learn a great deal more. Is there a way to go to a college to carry on with some of the things I am good at and possibly to start some new things which the school doesn't do?"

I paused for breath. Dad looked thoughtful, but he was smiling.

"I was hoping for something like that," he said. "You are clearly a bright lad and I wouldn't want you to end up in a dead end job. Have you thought what subjects you might like?"

I told him I had been exploring ideas. However, were they my ideas? They came into my head and mouth simultaneously as if 'Brain' had been waiting for this moment.

"Dad," I said, "I think I want to be an archaeologist or a geologist, or preferably where those two subjects meet."

For a moment there was silence as Dad stood there, trowel in hand with his mouth open.

"Well," he said, "I don't pretend to know what on earth you would be learning, let alone how you might earn a living, but you sound very certain and I imagine you've thought it out. You're not 15 yet so there's plenty of time, but I'm glad we've had this chat. Your mum and I will be relieved you have aims, even if we don't understand them."

We finished the planting in companionable silence. My mind however was buzzing.

After my weekend homework was done, that evening I stayed in my room largely staring at my cacti. The afternoon conversation had caught me unaware. Up to this point my cacti and more lately music, which 'Brain' had largely imposed on me, had been my main interests or hobbies I suppose.

I realised neither was leading to a career, but I wasn't worried. We had been told by the school, that 5 O Levels which included English, either language or literature, maths and 2 or 3 others, were a gateway to any profession, so long as one could be taken on by an employer and work one's way through the professional examinations, which may take 5 or 7 years. If one wanted to study at university, then a foreign language was required and I thought French was possible.

That night my thoughts were very different. Everything I had thought before was theory. Now my future seemed to have been laid out. It was inexplicable. What was this 'Brain' trying to do. I then thought, Wait a minute. It's not trying, it's going to succeed.

I remembered how I was quite unable to stop some of the more embarrassing outbursts. Could I resist these new ideas? Or were they plans? If so, who was doing the planning? It was the first time I had thought of 'Brain' being outside of myself. This was new.

I had better sleep on it, but again sleep that night would not come. My mind churned with new thoughts and some new thoughts were born. I needed to explore these. I would go first to the encyclopaedia by riding to my uncle's house and check on some ideas, just in case 'Brain' might cover its tracks.

I looked first for the idea that two minds might be capable of sharing thoughts. Several experiments were described and some had produced some unexplained results. This was called telepathy. Then I looked up things like prophecy in the hope of explaining the occasions when this had happened. This was less satisfactory, too many biblical quotes and very little about the present. I cut the word prophecy out and looked up "knowing the future". This was better, I saw the word 'precognition'. I knew enough to know it had Greek origins. Examples were given of things people had said which had turned out to be correct, but there were lots of cases when such were wide of the mark. I closed the heavy books and cycled home to my new house. My cousin Jim nor Uncle never asked what I was looking up thankfully.

That night I had more to go on and I began to review all of the episodes that had happened so far, in my mind.

Is there a pattern I thought. If 'Brain' is outside of me, generally trying to help me, then he must be quite clever and a great deal older than me. I decided he because he seemed to understand me so well. He obviously knew most of my thoughts, at least on these odd occasions when things had happened and yet it was one way only, I couldn't know his mind, only the bits he gave me. Generally, if I had asked 'Brain' a question, it had answered immediately. This felt creepy. He must be listening. But I could get no further and fell asleep.

Next day at breakfast I had another thought. 'He', as I now thought of 'Brain' as him, clearly knows the things I had predicted. Therefore 'He" was in the future looking back at me. This was all logical and the only thing that explained everything that had happened so far. Logical it may be, but it was not an explanation. After all, the future hadn't happened yet, surely? I couldn't ever discuss this with Dennis or anyone else. They would think I was crazy and the whole thing seemed like science fiction, something from the Eagle comic, Dan Dare and so on.

Nevertheless, I became more comfortable with my explanation and felt easier about my ability to keep 'Brain', I mean 'him', under control. So, I went to school as usual.

I enjoyed school now I was in the 4th year, as I had in the 3rds since the essay moment. Mr Dance still taught the English classes, though now we had to move to teachers' own rooms. So it was that day I had English.

At lesson's end, Mr Dance said, "Could I ask you to see me here after you have had your school dinner?"

I agreed of course. No one refused a teacher's request, however politely put. So, I turned up and was surprised to find Canon Rust there as well, plus Mr Viner and my geography teacher Mr Owen.

Crumbs! I thought they have been comparing notes. This is going to be tricky, but I tried to be as calm as I could. What was going to happen?

Mr Dance opened the conversation. This was not a surprise as I knew he was the senior teacher among the four of them. He said that he had been talking to the Head. I froze; this was not going to be good if the Head was involved in my affairs let alone my 'Brain'. I always felt that when the Head looked at you, which wasn't often I must admit, he could see right through you, thoughts and all.

I had only had the Head's attention twice since I entered the school. The first was an occasion in the third year when some of the more unruly boys had decided to play up the French teacher. He was a small Welshman who spoke French with a Welsh accent. I thought he was completely inoffensive and did not join in. This was not because I was a goody goody, but because I was rather sympathetic to the problem he had in discipline. He did not seem to be able to identify the culprits. To me they were pretty obvious. Also, if I'm honest there was the fact I was scared of being identified, which might have led to being expelled. The very next lesson after it had begun, the Head walked it. We stood, he left us standing and gave us a stony look, a bit like the stare of a gorgon. We almost turned to stone. He read the riot act and warned of dire consequences if there were to be a repeat.

The second occasion was very close to the first. The Head turned up to give us a complete lesson, no doubt to check our behaviour. We listened to him with total concentration. Unfortunately, there was piano music in my head and my fingers were tapping the desk as if playing a piano without me knowing it. He, however, spotted it.

"Windsor!"

I shot to my feet. "Sir?"

"Do you play the piano?"

"Er, no, Sir," I stuttered.

"Well, don't play the desk, and see Canon Rust afterwards and see if he can arrange lessons for you."

I didn't want any more frightening episodes like this. When the Head walked across the quad, everyone stopped what they were doing and a path cleared in front of him, a bit like the parting of the Red Sea, such was the respect and awe we held him in. He walked across never looking up and apparently unaware of any of us.

Mr Dance, watched by the other three, continued. "He allowed me to see your school records in quite a lot of detail, including your 11+ results. You may not be aware that these tests give you what is known as an IQ score. Are you familiar with this concept?"

I nodded. My lips were dry.

He carried on. "When you entered the school and were put into the alpha class you brought into the school a very high IQ score, one of the highest in some years." He paused. "We then examined your first year performance. We don't need to go into details. You had experiences which were not good and the Head was more than forgiving for the first two years while you slowly recovered. This was because he was aware of your potential. He has told me that he fully expected that you would eventually progress back to the alpha stream and he expressed surprise that you have shown little interest in this. Can I say, Freddie, that your "clever" plan to conceal your academic recovery by filling your work with deliberate mistakes to avoid perfect scores has fooled no-one. That's right, is it not, Mr Owen?"

Mr Owen with a grin said, "I rather enjoy seeing these errors; they are easy to spot and are sometimes bordering on the absurd. I have compared notes with Maths, French and so on and they all say the same, Freddie is holding back."

I'd been rumbled. What was coming next?

Mr Dance continued. "Well, now this is in the open, you can stop the nonsense, Freddie." He said in a very friendly way and I relaxed a little. "I am aware from talking to my colleagues that you possess some very unusual and advanced abilities, most notably in musical knowledge and in knowledge of art works."

Mr Viner nodded vigorously, again with a smile. I relaxed some more, but I thought, What do they want of me? That question was quickly answered.

"Why are you still in this stream with such exceptional abilities?"

Well, I couldn't tell what abilities came from me and those from 'Brain'. But was 'Brain' me all along? I was for the moment confused, but I had a straight question to answer.

"I am happy where I am, sir, and I enjoy my work," I said. "I have never wanted to re-join the alphas. I see no interest in their curriculum, particularly where it leads in terms of career."

I stopped and watched their faces, after all in this school this must be heresy? They were contemplating my words, so I continued.

"I must admit that in the first two years Latin was my particular bête noir. Now I love it because I can apply it to my interest in plants, even though we no longer have Latin lessons in the fourth year. Indeed, I see some Greek derivatives in some species. But the learning of the Punic wars has no appeal."

I stopped again and Canon Rust said, "Bête noir? Where did you pick that up and your knowledge of what the alphas are studying?"

I merely smiled, feeling more in control of this unusual meeting.

Mr Dance spoke again and revealed why this meeting had been called.

"We are anxious that, wherever you are in the school now, and you appear happy where you are, you will be contemplating your future. For instance, what will you do in the sixth form? My colleagues are here to give some guidance."

Nods from all the others and smiles; they had it all worked out I suspect. Mr Owen spoke and said that I would easily obtain a high score in geography and that he had spoken to maths who agreed that I would sail through both O and A level as well. Canon Rust interrupted saying that with a bit of guidance I could be put in for music since the curriculum at O level did not require an instrument.

"It would add to your O level score with little effort I suspect," he said, "and that is always a good investment, whichever way you are thinking."

I realised they were speaking to me as an adult in many ways. So I decided to respond in a similar way; I was no longer feeling any nervousness and was totally in control, at least that's how it felt at the time. I hope you don't think I was being big headed.

So, the various subjects were making bids for my A level time so as to enhance their reputations no doubt. They were in for yet more heresy from me shortly.

Mr Dance continued by saying, "I have been talking to some of your classmates and they all say they think you are brighter than you pretend. Helme calls you the class professor!"

I blushed, secretly pleased. I'd long admired Helme and now it was being reversed.

"Well, Freddie, what have you to say, have we been helpful in sorting your thoughts and guiding a possible career? By the way, have you thought about what you might like to do?"

This was the question which would put the cat among the pigeons, I thought.

I looked at each in turn. They were all looking very friendly, smiling rather self-satisfied smiles. I was aware that soon they would have to go off to their next class, as would I. Okay, this is it. Heresy is coming. I relaxed, it didn't matter how they took it, because it seemed I had been told what I was to do in future and no doubt some preparations had been made somehow and somewhere.

"I want to do either archaeology or geology as soon as possible and eventually anthropology, hopefully at university, so that I can work in a field where these subjects overlap. Without biology in the school, I feel that I should leave after O levels. I should seek a college where I can get closer to my aims and get an A level in biology, since this is essential for both aims."

I paused for a reaction.

Mr Owen spoke first. "What has biology got to do with either of your aims, Freddie?"

"Well," I said, "my interest in geology would be palaeontology and in archaeology the relationship of early civilisations to plants is obvious. In most sites plants leave traces, even though in my third year essay I said cacti didn't."

I grinned at Mr Dance.

"So, Freddie," he said, "you were playing with us even then."

Canon Rust added, "When you spoke of the Mozart symphonies, I realised you knew exactly how many he wrote. So you didn't fool all of us all the time, Freddie. By the way," he continued, "all this extra ability seemed to emerge in the third year rather suddenly. Some colleagues have described you as a late developer. Your 11+ gives the lie to that. You have always had ability, but were you aware of it?"

Again, I just smiled. I could not reveal my 'Brain" emergence on the day of the algebra homework.

"Well," said Mr Dance, "we all have work to do and the bell will go any minute. We all have things to think about so perhaps we can meet again when we have taken your replies into account. Thank you, Freddie, for being so honest and open with us, though I must say I was astonished at both your intentions and the erudition you have in expressing them. I feel we have all underestimated you yet again."

They left and I followed.

I went home on the bus that night and was pleased to do so because it gave me time to think about this new situation. I still had a year and a half in the school, as far as I was concerned, that is. 'Brain' may have had other ideas. I could no longer camouflage my abilities. But there was the question of my foresights. They had to be watched. Burning witches had gone out of fashion and I had no wish to see it brought back specially for me. I laughed out loud, fortunately no one on the bus noticed.

CHAPTER 5

I was under a spotlight in school and I knew it. Not comfortable! My lazy days were over; I had to be on my toes at all times. As I walked the half mile from the bus stop to home, I realised the teachers were not going to let this drop. One or other would try to pressurise me to accept the 'normal pathways'. How to resist when I didn't know how to achieve what I said I wanted to do? Mind you, I thought, I had said it with a conviction I may not have really felt. Tea was ready as usual, especially because the bus took longer than my bike. It was after all downhill all the way coming home.

I think I take my mum for granted, I thought, as I ate my tea. The kitchen was the warmest room in the house, most of the time. It had a range, a cooker fed on coke with a large and small oven and two hot plates on the top with lids on. My mum was very proud of this modern appliance. It could also heat two radiators, one in the hall and one on the landing to put some heat all over the house and heated towel rail in the bathroom. This gave a sense of luxury, something we had not had in our old house.

Both of my younger sisters always shared teatimes. Kate the youngest was only just five and Diana, we all called her Di, was eight. They both went to the local junior school, a walk of about one and a half miles. They were now considered old enough to go on their own so long as Di remembered to bring Kate home. They seemed the best of friends to me and I must admit they played little part in my life. Was I a bad brother? I don't think so. I listened to their chatter politely, but they had little understanding of my schoolwork or friends or thoughts. After tea they always scuttled off to watch the television set. This was a novelty because we had not long had it. It was bought just in time for the Coronation of the Queen. We had watched the funeral of King George on my Uncle Harry's set. Our set was actually on weekly rental because Dad had said the sets would be improved at a fast rate as more people got them. He was right because ours had a larger screen than my uncle's. It was in black and white and had only one channel. More channels were being promised in the future and some said that one day it might be possible to have colour as well. The girls loved to watch something called Muffin the Mule and the Flower Pot Men. I had more important things to think about.

My older sister had long left school and was working in a solicitors' office. Not bad I thought for one who had the early part of her education totally disrupted during the war. That thought put the Guernica painting back in my mind. I realised Mr Viner had been very quiet in the meeting, but very thoughtful. I felt the next art lesson could be interesting. I was not wrong.

Art was taught only two periods a week, so it was on the last double lesson on Friday that I next faced my favourite teacher. He was as kind and mild as ever. I was often amazed how he kept us unruly boys in control without ever raising his voice or giving any lines or detentions.

"Freddie," he said, "have you got a minute at the end of the lesson?"

I was on my bike that day so I had no reason not to agree to stay on. He invited me to sit at his desk. I remembered that he had made little input into the meeting we had recently had. I wondered what his ideas were going to be. He didn't have a strong interest in keeping me in an art A level. I wasn't that good. Good enough for O level and that would please him.

"I was interested in your proposed career pathways, Freddie," he said. "May I ask how you arrived at this unusual choice?"

It was put so politely and with such a genuine interest that I was off guard for a moment. What did I really know about geology or archaeology? Okay I had looked both up in the encyclopaedia when 'Brain' put the ideas in my head. I would have to flannel a bit, I thought.

"Well, Sir." I always answered teachers this way, it bought time. "They are both scientific professions."

"And have you ever met someone in any of them," he said, "a relative perhaps?"

"Er! No, Sir," I replied. "I have read about them and both appeal about equally, but the new science of anthropology is a very exciting field of discovery."

"Ah!" he said repeating me. "I think, you were a little more specific in our meeting, you seemed to have ideas about areas of overlap. I tell you, Freddie, that intrigued me. It suggested a great deal more knowledge than you seem to be revealing. We all know now how much 'cover up' you have engaged in over the past two, or is it four, years. I would like to know a little more of what is going on in your head. I feel that you have merely been offering us glimpses or more likely these have been coming out by accident. The detail with which you occasionally let us see suggests a knowledge base and intellect way above anything I have ever come across even in a grammar school of this standard. I sometimes think you are playing with us, Freddie."

I was blushing. I had never thought that I was doing this and I realised I must have been letting my guard down. Another explanation occurred. Maybe Mr Viner was gifted with unusual perception. That was a better thought, so I accepted it. It was easier to live with.

"I don't think I have been playing about, Sir," I said looking him in the eyes. "But I sometimes get confused."

He smiled, "Is there anything worrying you, Freddie?"

He looked me with a kindly gaze. At that moment I felt I could tell him everything, but something warned me that I daren't. It would not stay with him; he would probably tell at least some other teachers. I felt sorry that I had to keep up a deception. I knew he meant well and was trying to look after my best interests. He gave a sigh.

"All right, Freddie," he said. "Off you go, but remember you can speak to me in confidence about anything."

That was nice to hear, but still a risk I could not take at this time.

A couple of days later, Dennis and I were sitting on a bench behind the chemistry labs watching some of the boys kick a ball around the field which was now marked out for winter games rather than the summer cricket pitches. Dennis was quiet, but Dennis was always quiet, so when he spoke firmly it was a bit of a shock.

"Freddie, I have to tell you I am worried. Dash it all, you are not being straight with me. We have been friends since we were six. I'm your oldest and I hope best friend. You know you can trust me because I don't speak to many people. You chatter on to our group and I mostly watch and listen and remember things. What I want to say is, you have changed. It's more obvious to me than to the others because they don't know you so well as I do. I have watched you carefully for some time now and I can see that you are hiding things not only from us but teachers as well and I'll bet your parents. Am I right?"

I didn't reply because he hadn't finished.

He went on, "I think sometimes you have eaten an encyclopaedia for dinner and followed it with a dictionary for pudding. Some of the things you have come out with you could not possibly have come from the books you read nor what any teacher has taught you."

This was longest speech I had ever heard from Dennis and I felt that his concerns needed some explanation. But what? I had better come clean.

"It started in the third year," I said. "One day I woke up knowing I had my homework wrong and I knew the right answers. It was something in my head I think, but I don't understand what it was. I did wonder if I might be in danger of going mad, but the new thoughts keep coming and they don't seem to do me any harm. I have little control over them, but they seem to be in my best interests, so far anyway. I am sometimes, no, I'm always, bewildered by the knowledge I sometimes have. I have no idea where I get it honestly, Dennis. You will understand why I have to keep quiet and flannel a bit because I don't want to be thought any weirder than I already am."

This seemed a lame explanation, but it was all I could think of at the time.

Dennis was, however, more perceptive than I was giving him credit for. He had already said he spent time watching and listening to all of our chatter.

"If you have this odd or weird ability, Freddie, then you have the ability to get to the bottom of it and I can't believe you haven't tried." He looked at me hard.

I told him about the ideas of minds being twinned in telepathy and also about the ideas of precognition.

"Ah!" he said. "So, I am to be an accountant. I suppose that will please my dad. It explains your accurate prediction of teachers' absences. These can't be lucky guesses. If you know my future, why don't you know yours?"

I had no answer to that, but it did make me think.

At this point the afternoon bell went and we had to go to separate classes. I went with some relief. I had told Dennis as much as I could or dared and he had accepted it calmly, as he did with everything. I knew he would ask more when he had thought about my answers and I decided it was a great relief to have someone I could trust. I wasn't on my own anymore. But then would I ever be on my own while 'Brain' seemed to be organising my life?

Later that week, in a games lesson, I was chatting to other 'stragglers' on our patch of the field which was close to the music hut. The Canon passed by, saw me and beckoned me over. He obviously didn't have a class and I equally had no great purpose in aimless ball kicking, so I imagine he saw this as a golden opportunity to quiz me. I followed him to his music room and he sat at the piano as usual. He had put a chair nearby for me to sit on facing him. I was used to this grilling technique after the last meeting, but this was about music and I had greater confidence. I could reveal as little or as much as I wanted I thought.

"Let me see your hands," he said.

I was astonished. They were not as clean as I would have liked. I reddened as usual.

"Well," he said "they are potentially pianist hands. What would your parents say if we were able to arrange lessons for you?"

I thought about it. "Would there be a cost?" I asked.

"Well," he said, "pupils generally buy their own instruments and the cost is spread over their time in the school. But you already have a piano and no one ever buys those." He laughed. "The tuition is at present free, though it hasn't always been so."

"That's okay," I said. "My mum generally gives me what I ask for."

There was a long pause.

"Freddie, do you realise what you just said, and what it says about you?"

I realised that I had just declared I was a spoiled brat! There was no way out of this. It was to some extent true. No, it was a 100% true! I turned redder, I think, than I had ever been. This was a wake-up call. I would have to have a talk when I got home to change my ways big time. He saw my embarrassment and didn't want to pursue it.

"Freddie, can we do a little experiment because I am interested in several aspects of your gift?"

Well, no one had called 'Brain' a gift before, I thought. I nodded.

He proceeded to rattle off the openings of various symphonies and concertos by a mixture of composers. I identified each with ease and eventually had the nerve to say, "Sir, this is too easy. I am sure that many folk can identify the opening bars of famous works such as these."

He stopped and looked at me. "I'm sure you're right about adults, but not necessarily a boy of your age. Well, as you wish, we'll try something harder."

He repeated the process, but taking extracts from other works. I was actually amazed at his prowess. He was able to do so much from memory. Maybe my abilities were common to all musicians?

Again, I managed to identify most. There was one piece that nearly floored me.

"I think it's by a Russian composer called Shostakovich," I said. "He is still alive and I know the Russian leader Stalin favours his music. I actually find his music not to my taste, so I have not explored it."

"Remarkable," said the Canon.

"So," said the Canon, "you actively explore music. How do you do that?"

"Well, Sir." There it was again, standard buying time. "I now have my sister's wireless as well as her record player and so I can listen to the BBC Third Programme with all the concerts."

"Freddie," said the Canon, "I accept some of what you say, but I find it hard to see how you have learned so much in what is apparently a short space of time."

I didn't reply to this. There was no rational answer.

"Tell me," he said, "is music in your head all of the time?"

I could answer this honestly.

"No, Sir, not when I'm having ordinary lessons or doing homework, but when I cycle or bus home, when I'm out walking or even in the school breaks, then it's always there."

"Do you select what you hear?"

"No, Sir, it just comes."

"And how do you hear it, the basic tune, or more?"

"No, Sir, I hear all of the parts, every instrument or orchestral section coming in, the tempo and the crescendos and diminuendos. Everything, Sir."

"Remarkable," he said.

He looked at me for a long time saying nothing.

"Freddie, do you realise that many of our great musical conductors would give anything for this gift, if what you tell me is true. They have to set hours aside to learn pieces and then decide how they will interpret them and your mind seems to be able to do this with little effort. I wonder." He paused. "I wonder if I could do a little experiment to verify your claim."

"I'm not claiming, Sir," I said indignantly. "I'm just saying how it is. I don't understand it, Sir, but I do enjoy it."

"Quite so," the Canon said. "Calm down, Freddie. I did not mean to upset you. I have one more question for the time being. This has been going on in your head for about eighteen months, since the third year?"

"Yes, Sir," I said. "It started early in the third year and has grown more intense since. I don't know where it came from, but I enjoy it and I've done my best with records and the wireless."

"Yes, I see that, Freddie, but I wonder how it is you are able to remember so much of each piece apparently on first hearing. Is this the case?"

"Yes, it is, Sir. Mostly I only need to hear a piece once and I have it all in my mind and it stays there."

"Remarkable," the Canon said.

I decided to reveal one more thing, whether it would make things better, worse or clearer, I had no idea.

"It's not just music, Sir."

He looked hard at me. "Go on," he said.

"It's everything, Sir. Everything I hear, see, read, everything in every lesson. I don't, in fact, think I can forget anything. Not that I try," I added in a quiet voice.

"Remarkable!" he said it again.

I thought I had lost count how many times he had said it. Actually, for me that was now impossible, he had said it four times.

"Well," he said, "you will have to go now, the afternoon is drawing to a close, but thank you for opening up and being so frank and honest in your answers."

I left and went back to the changing rooms to join the others. There were one or two curious boys of course, but when I said in a bored tone, "Oh! We just talked music." They lost interest. On the way home I did wonder what form the Canon's 'experiment' might take. Will he go ahead with it and would I like it?

I realised I had not told the whole truth about my memory. I did remember a lot, but not everything. I had come to the conclusion that my memory was selective. Much I heard that did not interest me I pushed to one side and I suppose I could recall it, but generally I knew I didn't need to.

Next time I saw Dennis, I asked him whether he saw me as a spoiled brat?

He looked at me hard. "Where's that come from?" he said.

"Well," I said, "it's something I said to the Canon and it's been worrying me."

"Ah," he said, "the Canon does seem to be able to hit the nail on the head."

"But you're my friend," I said. "If I was, you wouldn't be surely?"

"It might be that I am your tolerant friend," he said with a smile. The smile helped.

"Seriously," I said, "what do you really think?"

He laughed. "Well, you do have the best bike in the school, and your uniform is always smart. But you don't get any more pocket money than the rest of us. You get the going rate, five shillings. So I don't suppose you take your parents for granted any more than most of us. But if your conscience is tweaking you, you can change."

"Hang on," I said, "your uniform is always as new as mine when it's needed!"

"Ah," he said, "but my conscience is clear."

"Okay," I said, "but you will tell me if you detect 'bratishness'?"

"I most certainly will, and I will fine you a shilling." That was Dennis alright. He went on, "Look, your parents want to do their best for you, agreed?"

I nodded.

"So long as you don't take advantage and ask for unreasonable things or things you don't really need, you're not a brat."

I relaxed. Gosh, this kid is wise, I thought.

I hadn't had the talk with my folks and now I didn't need to. That reminded me that they hadn't had 'the talk' with me. I think you probably know which one. I was glad because neither I, nor they, could have coped with the embarrassment. Anyway, as far as I was concerned it was too late. I knew some or most, I'm not sure which, from chats with close friends and overheard conversations of older pupils. I expect I had some things wrong, but oddly 'Brain' was not helping me out on this topic. Time would tell.

CHAPTER 6

I haven't told you about one of the strangest things that happened at school. We had a cadet force. Yes really! Every Thursday we dressed in soldiers' uniform to go to school and in the afternoons of Thursdays we paraded, drilled and did army exercises and weapons training.

Our uniforms had to be carefully pressed with sharp creases, our boots had to shine like mirrors. Our belts had to be 'blancoed', with badges and buckles polished till they gleamed. We had to do it all ourselves, said the RSM. Yes, we had a real life genuine Regimental Sergeant Major who was really the force behind the force. He could be very stern with minor or major faults in our appearance.

I knew from my cousins and others who had gone to other schools that this was something that only our school did. I suppose it was a hangover from the pre 1945 Education Act when the school had come into the state system. It had brought all of the old customs with it. Of course, during the war, which was still affecting everyday life, it would be very useful to have a ready supply of trained people capable of becoming non-commissioned staff and officers. Anyway, that seemed to be the intent of everything we did on Thursday afternoons. I don't think most of us minded really. It was exercise, much was interesting and we realised that many of the teachers, now parading as officers, were actually soldiers in the war. It certainly gave them more respect, I think. How does this affect my story? Well, I'll tell you.

Once a year the whole cadet force, and that really meant the whole school above the second year, went on a training day on Cannock Chase near the Rifle Range where we had earlier learned to fire .303 bullets to distant targets. Well, on this particular day we loaded onto motor buses which were on the road outside school, all in uniform, of course. All teachers who were officers, and that was most of them, spread themselves around the buses. Off we went.

Dennis was sitting next to me as was to be expected. I began have an uneasy feeling about this trip which grew the closer we got to the destination. The journey took about an hour. A picture began to appear in my mind, a picture of a disaster in which three boys would be badly hurt. This would happen today I knew. Had I been given this foresight in order to prevent it?

The coaches unloaded and we formed up in platoons, about 30 in each with 3 sections of 10. We were marched to the armoury by the shooting range and issued with rifles that had firing pins. Our usual ones at school did not have these, of course, and were perfectly safe. These were not. We were then given a demonstration of how dangerous a blank could be at close range, as an officer fired at a tin can and blew a hole in it even though there was no bullet. Then our platoon sergeant, a sixth form boy whom we knew, gave each of us 5 blank .303 cartridges. We were to use these in various ways during the exercise, but never at close range. Next, we were given an arm band. Ours was blue and we were to be the attacking group. The green bands were given to other platoons who were to defend a headquarters' hut some distance away. Dennis and most of my friends were together in our company of ten simply because we had come off the coach together. Our sergeant, on orders from a teacher who was a lieutenant, told us to find a concealed place and watch to the west and wait for further orders.

By now my feeling of imminent disaster had grown and I knew now exactly who was involved. My mind had a clear picture. However, I also knew that the plot they had would take place towards the end of the day. I had time to work out what to do. I also knew I could not reveal my ability to foresee the future to anyone new. Only Dennis knew about this ability, so he must be persuaded to spoil the plot.

We were lying in a series of sandy hollows, well suited to the exercise, and the vegetation around was scrubby thorn and bracken. Good concealment should the defenders become attackers. This was almost certainly what they would be encouraged to do. The object of the game was to capture opponents' armbands or capture the headquarters. I doubt anyone thought that was possible though.

Time passed and we saw no one. Neither an officer nor a sergeant came to see what we were doing nor give further orders. We heard shouts and occasional rifle fire and sometimes heavier weapons fired, no doubt in a very safe direction. There were some very loud bangs and I thought some of the professional soldiers supervising the whole thing had let off some thunder-flashes to simulate hand grenades, all very colourful I thought. I wriggled over to Dennis and told him what I knew was going to happen. I thought we had about half an hour to foil it. He knew enough about the three lads in my class to realise this was not an impossible idea. He also knew the accuracy of previous "prophecies".

"I think," I said, "if you found our sergeant and said you had heard them bragging on the coach, he would believe you. You must make him swear he will not reveal how he found out. I don't want you or me to be a victim of their revenge later. I believe that they will gave away their location by making a small fire, thinking it won't show among all this chaos. You might spot this smoke, Dennis, and then he will have to investigate. What they are going to do is throw all of their blanks onto the fire to make one almighty bang. There are six of them, but three are really just daft hangers on. I hope they get away.

What five of them don't know is that one has found or stolen three live rounds. This is the danger and bearing in mind bullets can travel nearly a mile, someone could be killed. An officer needs to know this. Don't say how you know the detail because they will forget details in their panic to stop it. They are bound to understand the danger to themselves and the boys involved."

Dennis crawled away to find our sergeant. I lay there hoping I had done enough. Eventually Dennis returned and reported all had gone well. The lads had a bad reputation with prefects and he had needed no convincing of the likelihood of the plot. Dennis said the sixth form sergeant had gone immediately to find the lieutenant. We could do no more.

I cautiously raised my head and looked in the direction where a small bluish whisp of smoke was getting thicker.

Suddenly I heard orders being given, scurrying noises and then one huge explosion. Then, for a while, silence. I had a cold feeling, but then I remembered that the foreknowledge was to prevent disaster. Soon, further commands and the sound of folk being marched away. No panics, no calls for a stretcher party, so it had worked out. I felt relief. I saw Dennis looking at me with what looked like awe on his face. No one else had noticed what we doing and we resumed our watching and waiting.

The time left was inconclusive. No one came near us and eventually we decided we would shoot our five blanks into a nearby innocent thorn bush. Then the whistles blew signifying the end of the exercise. We formed up and marched as smartly as we could to the headquarters. This was exactly as we had left it so clearly uncaptured. All in all, a very odd experience.

We were given hot tea by the army personnel. Very welcome and I noticed the gang of three sitting with a prefect/ sergeant standing close by. No doubt their fate would be decided back at school. I felt no guilt nor sorrow for them; someone could have been killed or badly injured. They seemed incapable of understanding the consequences of their actions. Well, they would now, I was sure.

I was pleased that the three ringleaders were on their own. The other hangers-on must have been sufficiently far away from the fire to get away. I knew that they weren't bad, simply easily influenced. Well, they had a useful wake-up call today.

On the journey home Dennis was in the seat next to me as always. He spoke in a low voice, but really that didn't matter with all the chatter and singing of fairly rude songs on the coach.

"This is highly significant," he said. "It's a very different sort of 'talent' you have revealed today."

I replied, "I was sorry to involve you, Dennis, but you will understand why it was necessary, won't you?"

"Yes," he said, "I was happy to do it and I had no doubt about your foresight, extraordinary though it was, or rather is."

"I was actually rather surprised that you agreed."

I said looking him in his eyes for an honest reaction. He thought for a while.

"Well, I have heard of people having this experience and there was something about you, the way you looked and spoke which said you clearly believed it. Also, I knew you would not ask me to do something stupid which would rebound on me."

I was quite touched by Dennis's faith in me, after all I had been filled with all sorts of doubts, confusion and so on for months.

CHAPTER 7

Dennis - I have known Freddie for a long time. I remember I was very nervous when I changed junior schools, even though they were about the same distance to walk, but not all of my class were moved with me. I'm very shy and didn't have many friends. We were taken to the dining room, the school hall actually, and there was empty place on a bench and I sat down by a boy who was almost as small as I was. I looked at the boy, he seemed nice. He was obviously as shy as I was. He looked at me and smiled. I felt a warm feeling go through me.

"Hello," he said.

I don't think I would have had the courage to talk to him. A strange impulse made me say, "Will you be my friend?"

"Yes," he said.

It seemed to be a contract because we did become friends, apparently for the rest of our lives possibly. Certainly, it lasted through the junior school and into the grammar school and I always sought Freddie out in the free times. Now, however, I wondered if I knew Freddie as well as I thought I did.

Freddie had been doing and saying some weird stuff lately. I wasn't sure I understood him, but I had always understood him in the past. I had been with him for so long. I had played with him at weekends, I had been to his birthday parties and he to mine for years. We had talked about stuff we would not share with anyone else, like his 'brat' worries. We were soul mates. But who was this new Freddie I didn't recognise? I would have to have a talk to find out what was going on in his head. I felt that it was important that I got to the bottom of this weird stuff.

Freddie - That night there was no homework and I spent most of the evening in my room trying to work out what had happened and how and mostly who.

I wondered sometimes what Canon Rust was plotting for me, but not too worried. I accepted I would probably cope whatever it was. In fact, I didn't have to wait long. Surprisingly it was revealed in art about a week later.

"Could I have a word after the lesson?" said Mr Viner.

Because it was last lesson on a Friday there was never a reason to say no, so long as I was again on my bike. The class was by now used to my little chats with Charlie and they took no notice as they filed out.

Charlie said, "I don't think I'm breaking any confidences by telling you of a conversation I had with Mr Dance and Canon Rust in the staffroom today. Indeed, both agreed I should sound you out for your reactions. We think Mr Rust's idea is astonishing but has some built in safeguards so that you will not be exposed to embarrassment or ridicule."

I was silent. What was this thing that could potentially do this to me? I was not keen to look a fool in front of anyone, let alone the possibility of a wider audience.

Charlie went on, "The Canon will explain the details to you unless, of course, you make it clear to me that this scheme is not on. However, the gist is this, you appear to have an unusual gift in that you are able to remember every note in a piece of music, possible on first hearing. The Canon will test this in private, so that you are comfortable. What he is suggesting is that this will be followed with a musical piece performed by the school orchestra, that you will conduct a piece which you will have a large say in selecting. Then as a reward, if this goes well, you will conduct the orchestra at the next speech day or Christmas concert in a month's time or some such. Well, what do you think?"

I was silent for some time while I absorbed this. Charlie was patient and didn't speak. Oddly, the only thing I could come out with was, "It will have to be a concerto not a symphony, something within the orchestra's ability and something that a soloist can excel at."

"That's between you and others," said Mr Viner and I went home with my mind in a spin.

Oddly, I was not frightened of the task, only the problem of finding a piece that met the conditions. I found my mind focused on that only. It will be a piano concerto, I thought. Mr Rust's solo abilities are not in doubt and something with a strong theme that the pupils in the orchestra will enjoy.

I realised I had no idea of their repertoire, nor their standard. They were made up of boys of all years and I assumed that the younger ones might provide me with a problem. I dismissed the thought as pompous on my part. It was the Canon's job to ensure they could cope collectively. They would have plenty of time to prepare because I had a choice of dates and the concert would be when I was in the fifth form.

About a week later, the Canon again called me to a meeting. This time only himself and as usual it was in the music hut. He opened the conversation with, "I thought I would give to time to think about my proposal."

"I'm happy with it," I said.

"Have you thought of a piece?"

"Yes," I said, "I think Grieg's Piano Concerto No 1 in A."

"Your reasons for this?" he asked.

"Well," I said, slightly embarrassed, "I know you can play pretty well anything, but this concerto in my mind has two big advantages. First, it starts almost with the solo piano, apart from the drum roll; the orchestra is brought in later. Second the orchestral piece is inherently tuneful which the orchestra will enjoy. Also," I added, "there are significant roles for the woodwind and brass. There are bound to be experienced players here, thanks to the cadet band."

The Canon smiled at this cheeky comment.

"I like your reasoning," he said, "but I think in view of the time period maybe we should limit the performance?" This was clearly a suggestion.

"Absolutely," I said. "I suggest the first movement."

He agreed.

"Will the string section cope?" I said, remembering that I had never heard the orchestra perform. "The strings and the brass and woodwind are all rather exposed in this piece. Will they be able to cope?

"I think you will have to trust me," he said.

I realised he was speaking to me as a colleague not a pupil. It was an odd realisation and an odd sensation.

"Right!" he said. "That's the plan, now let's get down to detail. First, I want to play a piece of reasonable complexity on my gramophone that you will conduct as if an orchestra is in front of you. You may choose the piece and I will find the record. Any thoughts? You will not have to worry about the capabilities of a national orchestra."

We both laughed at this quip. My mind raced and I came out with Mendelssohn's Violin Concerto in E last movement.

"And the reason?" said the Canon.

"Well," I said, "it is the admixture of the violin with the orchestra which plays a subordinate role, but the sheer excitement of the crescendos at the end."

"I can't argue with that," he said.

The meeting finished with an agreement he would test my ability at a date to be decided and the rest of the plan would depend on his verdict. I was somewhat bewildered by what was now developing.

So, it happened in due course we met in the music room. I faced the gramophone and he sat behind it facing me. He had given me a small rostrum or stand to elevate me above the theoretical orchestra. It happened to be a new recording of Fritz Kreisler with the London Philharmonic Orchestra. I was in awe. I had never heard this one. Recorded in 1950 it had only reached the shops a couple of years ago and was still very expensive

The Canon put one of the new diamond styluses onto the gramophone and gently lowered it onto the start of the third movement. I was excited by the interplay between the violin and the orchestra, Of course, as in my target piece, the Grieg, I was not to conduct the soloist, but here the orchestra was almost always in the background. I don't know whether I was setting the exciting tempo or the violins, but I was concentrating on the violins especially at first. Oddly, I felt I was bringing in the sections which, of course, I wasn't really. I was sure not to fall behind on any entries. We came all too soon to the tremendous crescendos and the final crashing chords and the sudden cut off.

I was sweating. I had lost myself even though I had never heard this superb rendition; I was in a world of my own. Mostly my eyes were shut. I had no need to refer to the score. Not that it would have made any sense since I had never learned to read music, but the score was in my mind, every note and every pause and nuance that the composer had intended. At that moment I felt as if I was the composer. Later I felt this was cheeky.

I thought when I was at home, this is the biggest thing that I will have ever done. Am I up to it? Oddly I felt confident, though goodness knows why. Perhaps 'Ignorance is bliss' as the old saying goes.

We met again in the music hut by arrangement. I was beginning to feel at home in this place.

"I have had an idea," I said.

"So have I," Canon Rust said "You first, Freddie."

"Well," I said, "I have been listening again to the last movement and I can't bear to see the piece dissected."

"Stop!" said the Canon. "That is what I was about to say. We should play the whole piece."

"But," I said, "what about the players?"

He interrupted me, "Again, leave that to me. I have an idea. I shall invite one or two friends and some of the seniors from the girls' high school. Will that put more pressure on you, Freddie?"

"I don't think so," I said. "But what will they think when they see someone my age coming onto the rostrum?"

The Canon chuckled.

"From my piano I look forward to seeing their faces. However, the main orchestra could have a rehearsal with you if you wish."

"No," I said with little thought, "it's best if all rehearsals are done by yourself."

"Well, I can't do that and play the piano," he laughed.

"No, I suppose not."

"Don't worry, I have a stand in, so the practices need not concern you. In fact, this conversation means we can keep your appearance secret until the night. You will be advertised as a guest conductor. I have every confidence in your strange ability, Freddie, and I am willing to stick my neck out, as you might say."

I went home and thought it all over. I had access to a recording of the concerto played by Percy Grainger. It was already old, but I could pick out the bones of the piece.

Following a dramatic drumroll, the piano opens first with octaves sweeping the keyboard from top to bottom, followed by an ascent of giant arpeggios. It is so dramatic, I thought, it will grab the orchestra as they wait to come in on my command, I meant signal, but I was getting carried away by the power this experience was giving me.

Another thought came to me, this 'Brain' business! I hadn't given much thought to 'him' lately. It was obvious that he was trying to and succeeding in helping me with schoolwork and had apparently a career pathway thought out for me. However, I could not understand why so much music was in my mind since that first day when I needed help in maths. My lack of experience with an instrument ruled out a career here, so why had I been led down this pathway to conducting an orchestra? I was surely not going to do this ever again.

There were no answers, so my thoughts returned to the music. The main theme is announced by the cellos and the second movement starts with a gentle folk melody with the violins almost singing. I hoped the younger ones didn't get too enthusiastic here. I wondered about the trumpet and woodwind exposure. Then introduced by piano trills the piano leads to the finale where virtuoso playing must stand out. I had heard the Canon playing many pieces when he was testing me and I supposed I may have no fears here, but I wondered. No, I thought, he has never shown any doubt since I suggested the piece. I realised how little we pupils knew about our teachers and their accomplishments, so wrapped up were we in our small lives. It was a sobering thought and it put me in my place.

CHAPTER 8

Dennis and I were sitting on the benches behind the Science labs as usual during the lunch hour and I decided to open up and tell him the thoughts I'd had the previous evening lying on my bed. I had no idea if these were my thoughts or whether 'Brain' had decided the time was right for them.

I told Dennis that I had been contemplating the nature of time.

"What?" he said. "What do you mean?"

"Well," I said, "is time a straight line? Look, a) you're born, b) then we're here at school, c) then we leave and have a career, perhaps get married and have children, d) then we retire and live a few years, e) if time is like a railway track we hit the buffers and that's that."

"I suppose that's right," Dennis said.

"Well," I said, "suppose time is even more like a railway track. Our lines run alongside when we are in school, but when we go home there are points in the track, we go our separate ways and other tracks are alongside."

"Okay," Dennis said, "where is this leading?"

"Well," I said and continued with the remainder of the

ideas I'd had. "The points allow changes and possibly choices, but the tracks go only one way. Okay?"

"Okay," said Dennis.

"So, when we both leave school next year the points may determine we never see each other or anyone else from school again."

"I suppose that's possible," Dennis said.

"There again," I said. "I have had the foreknowledge that our tracks will coincide from time to time."

"I'm glad of that," said Dennis.

"Now," I said, "for my most interesting thought. All the tracks, everyone's individual tracks face one way and there is only one ultimate direction. So, we get past present and future."

"Okay," said Dennis, "with you so far."

"Well," I said, "for present folks to meet up in the future, which is almost bound to happen, then there must be bends in the lines between the points, ok?"

"Yes, I suppose so," he said.

"Now suppose one track could loop round and come close to my track and suppose this was my own track. It doesn't contradict time because it is still in the future. The person, possibly me, has still got his life experiences behind him and of course is much older and more experienced, but because of this loop is able to come alongside my track and talk across the line. Yes?"

"I don't see why not," Dennis said, "but it must be very rare."

"Just as well," I said, "but it does explain what has been happening, doesn't it?"

"I did say that this 'Brain' as you call it would help you to work it out, didn't I?"

"Yes," I said, "but I wasn't very confident until last night."

The bell went and we went our separate ways, but I felt much better having sorted my thoughts out and having confided in Dennis who seemed to accept my theory.

Schoolwork and routines filled my time for the next few weeks and term came to an end. Then I was in the fifth form. Everything seemed the same. No one mentioned the exams after next Easter, not for the whole of the year as far as I remember. They were simply taken for granted. Therefore, there were no worries about them. I had continued to grow taller to my satisfaction and I was more or less the same as most in the class. Dennis was more or less the same. Being called shrimps was a thing of the past. In fact, I realised it was about three years since a prefect had used the term.

In art Charlie told us that in the forthcoming exam next year, we had a choice between life drawing and church architecture. Very few of us fancied drawing each other, but Charlie explained that for the exam he would provide someone we didn't know. I and about half the class chose church architecture and Charlie promised us a week's trip to the Cotswolds to see examples first hand. I think that this was the first time this sort of thing had happened in the school in 500 years. We all had to join the YHA first and I did straight away. It was a distraction and a pleasant one even though it would not happen till the Easter holidays. By then I would have had my sixteenth birthday. However, the concert had been changed from speech day or some other of the usual calendar events, to a thing in its own right. An invitation concert, the school's first. This should have 'freaked me out', I thought. Then I thought, I have never heard that term. Did 'Brain' put it there? Is it from the future I wondered? Well, it seemed appropriate and anyway I was not 'freaked out', I was surprisingly calm.

As the concert time came close, I had meetings with the Canon where he explained the etiquette of conducting. How first on stage is the 'concertmaster', in our case first violin. She will organise the note to which the whole orchestra will tune. Only then will we go up onto the platform together, we will bow to audience, the orchestra will probably stand up, though there may be an element of shock, I thought and laughed to myself.

"At this point you would normally shake hands with the leader, but I will cut that out," he said.

To spare her blushes, I thought. He would take his place at the piano and I onto the rostrum. I face the audience still and then I turn and indicate the orchestra to sit.

"There will be a pause until you are sure they are ready; they will show you this by their stillness. You will look to me and I will nod. I don't have to tell you I'm sure that the soloist sets the tempo for most of a concerto unlike a symphony."

I nodded. I knew this, though how I don't know.

"In the orchestra the players will be following their own music, the less experienced rigidly, the more experienced, will glance at you from time to time. The first violin all the time; she is your best ally in time keeping. But don't worry, the music has a way of taking over the conductor and the orchestra."

He smiled and I saw he was looking forward to the event as much as I was. Finally, he reminded me that concerti were written in three parts, though there were no noticeable breaks in this one to complicate things.

About three weeks before, he met me again and said, "Freddie, what are you going to wear?"

I had to confess I hadn't given this a thought. He told me what conductors usually wore, though I knew this from pictures in books and newspapers.

"This would not be appropriate for someone of your age, even second hand, and I doubt we could find anything to fit," he said.

"I could ask my mum for a suit for my sixteenth birthday," I said.

"Yes," he replied, "that would be appropriate. Choose a dark colour, black would be best or dark blue perhaps, either will be appropriate for all sorts of things in your future, college interviews and such. A white shirt such as you wear to school, but make it a new one; if you tell Halls in the town it's for a special occasion, they will be helpful I'm sure. You will need to show cuffs and cuff links. Be sure not to describe the occasion; we don't want the secret to get out, do we? Finally, a bow tie; this will set you off from the rest, I think. I will get one and tie it for you because it can be tricky, but you will be able to keep it for future occasions."

What future he was thinking for me I have no idea, but it was extremely unlikely that 'Brain' would put me through this again. Then I had the thought, OK, what will he have in store, and why this anyway?

My mum thought a suit for my coming birthday was a good idea, though she said I might grow a little more it could last for a year or two. She always thought like that; everything was to last in her view. So, we went to the shop which each year had supplied school uniform parts I had needed as I grew. It was a general tailor as well, so I was able to choose to some extent. My parents were partly in on the secret, though I had sworn them to secrecy, so the suit was suitable. I chuckled at the pun.

It was to be an invitation concert though most tickets went to parents of pupils, staff and their friends, governors; certain town dignitaries were invited so the front rows would be taken up by faces I didn't know. Of course, parents of all of the pupils in the orchestra from both schools would be well represented, so we found out it was a sell-out. The tickets did acknowledge the mixed orchestra, the soloist was Canon Rust and D. Mus. and D.D. appeared after his name, I was described anonymously as guest conductor. It did raise queries, but none were answered; this in itself was curious and people said so.

On the day before the concert, I made a point of catching the Canon on his way to his room.

"Sir," I said, "tympani at the beginning?"

"Absolutely."

I said, "That first drum roll before your crashing chords?"

He looked at me, "Are you getting cold feet, Freddie?"

"Not in the least," I said.

"You do trust me with my orchestra, don't you, Freddie?"

I was a little crestfallen. He softened his looks and tone.

"It's all in hand. The orchestra will be up your expectations. I understand you only listen to the best, eh?"

I relaxed. "Sir, do I look at the players during your solo parts to check they are waiting for their entry?"

"Of course, Freddie, they get a lot of confidence from seeing that you are aware of every section. They will be expecting great things from you, as are we all."

With these words in my mind, I prepared for the evening of the big day.

Of course, the concert had been arranged for a Saturday night, so that more folks would be free to come, so I had the day to prepare. It was odd, I was putting all my faith in a disembodied entity called 'Brain', whom I now more than suspected might be me in the future. I had been led down this path and could not believe it would end in disaster and massive embarrassment. Why would 'Brain' do that to me? For the last two and a half years I'd had nothing but good things. I had learned so much, gained so much confidence. I felt all this was for a reason. Anyway, I was determined to enjoy both the experience and the music. Mostly the music, I told myself. Something I had a part in creating in partnership with the Canon. I knew he was going to enjoy it, he had told me so, though I was never allowed to hear him practising. I had asked him about this and he said, "I have a better piano at home and the school's concert grand is in the public eye all day". I accepted this explanation.

We had an early tea and the family began to dress up. My two younger sisters were considered too young to come, so an uncle and aunt were going to 'babysit'. My big sister was coming, but was somewhat sceptical. My parents were looking smart. I rarely saw my dad in a suit. This was not his demob suit, I thought, it's much better fitting. My mum had a new coat. They were all going by car, but the Canon was picking me up earlier.

So, I was in my new togs and rather than look odd I put on my school tie. I could see why I was to have a bow tie eventually because it didn't look right. The front door bell had me waiting for it, so I opened immediately.

After a brief introduction of the family, the Canon said, "Don't worry, Freddie will be fine; he has talents which few of us understand."

I looked at my big sister, she was clearly not convinced. It took only a few minutes to get to school and we entered by a door no pupils were allowed to enter. We had time to spare, though when we went nearer to the stage by a circuitous route, I could hear the chatter of the players. Some musical sounds came as well as they tuned.

The Canon excused himself and said he must change. In no time it seemed he returned in his tails and white bow tie. He tied my black bow tie for me and I regarded this new Freddie in a mirror. There was a confidence and a smile in my face.

"Remember the etiquette on the platform that we have discussed," he said, "but don't worry, I can whisper to you later on."

I peeped through a curtain. The stage was larger than usual because the rear curtain was drawn aside; this was where scenery was when plays took place. There was a larger orchestra than I was expecting. I noted three cellos and two trumpets. In the far left corner an impressive drum section. The

Canon brought me back to reality. A hush from the audience and a lady I didn't know walked past us. The leader I was told. Applause broke out which she acknowledged. She began tuning the orchestra.

While waiting a little longer, I noticed that the stage lighting was on, flooding the stage while the hall was in semi darkness; I could hardly make out anyone. One less distraction I thought.

"Right, we are on," said the Canon and we walked onto the stage.

The clapping was as enthusiastic as for the first violinist had been, but I suspected mainly for the soloist whom everyone knew.

I made the ritual bows both to the soloist and the audience and acknowledged the leader who had brought the orchestra to their feet. I knew it was my job to indicate that they sit and with both hands I did. They were all looking at me, but I expected this, soon they would be too busy. I picked up my baton from the lectern and looked at the leader. She smiled and indicated she was ready and I looked at the Canon who smiled and nodded. We were off.

I looked over to the percussion; he stared back in anticipation with sticks poised. My baton pointed and the tremendous drumroll filled the hall. It was ended exactly as the piano's spectacular chords and arpeggios filled the hall. I watched the players and they came in with the strings exactly as I wanted.

My heart sang at the beauty of it and my arms had a mind of their own. We came to a section where the piano played quietly and I felt the players were over- enthusiastic. My left hand signalled diminuendo. It happened and I knew I was in charge. Both arms were sweeping in time as I set the tempo. The cellos and woodwind developed the theme again, the piano reiterating it. A solitary horn called; I had brought him in exactly. Clarion calls from the brass and the piano trilled from top to bottom of the keyboard. I was in another world. The theme gained pace and volume on piano, with much of the orchestra silent, waiting. I watched for their entry. The first movement ended with the same chords which had introduced the piece.

The next section gave me more to do as the violins and cellos dominated the new theme. There were exposed parts for violin and horn. They were all watching near their entry. The piano was gentler now and the orchestra a constant background. Then woodwind followed by brass as the power grew. Flute and French Horn called over the piano, then the movement ended with six ascending notes.

A brief pause and the piano picked up pace. I was working hard now everything was happening so fast and so dramatically; the orchestra responded as excitement grew. The pace on the piano became astonishing. A melody on flute brought calm and the strings picked up the theme. For a while everything was calmer as the piano developed the theme. For a moment there was a pause and the piano began the lilting theme which would end the piece. The orchestra chased the piano in turn, pace and volume increasing. The orchestra took over for a while, building volume with every section involved, the lilting theme on piano again faster and faster, I felt the excitement as the pace and complexity increased. The players brought back the theme at a slow but powerful pace, the piano interrupted them and they repeated the dominant theme, then the three final chords and silence.

I was breathless, what an experience. What a beautiful powerful musical piece. But I was forgetting my role.

I think the power of the piece had affected everyone. Some seconds passed. It seemed an age and the applause began. I smiled at the players and turned to the crowd. The next few minutes were a blur. I remembered to shake hands with the Canon and we bowed to the crowd. I remembered too to bring the orchestra to their feet by section and finally together and so on, everything I had been coached in. Eventually we left to more clapping.

I turned the Canon and I said "Sir, you were brilliant."

"You are wondering, are you, Freddie?" he said. I had to admit I was. "I went to music college many years ago and had a brief career as a soloist," he said. "Look we must go back on" and so we did.

The orchestra were still on their feet and I realised they were applauding me as well as the Canon. We both took a bow in acknowledgement. My heart was pounding, my face flushed. It was hard to realise it was all over. As the orchestra sat the audience realised we were not taking another encore and there was a general shuffling and excited conversations could be heard.

We stood for a while, to recover I think.

"Well, Freddie you didn't let me down either."

We laughed.

I was to go home with my parents. In the car, they were silent, but mum was making extensive use of her hanky. Her only comment was, "That was lovely." Dad grunted so I supposed he was agreeing. Jean spoke. "Well, Freddie, where did that come from?"

I gave my stock answer, "I read a lot and I stole your gramophone." She looked hard at me and we went home in silence.

In the house my aunt and uncle were waiting.

"Was it successful?" they said together. They had little idea what had happened.

"Yes!" said my family in unison, "very."

"Why are you dressed as a penguin?" said my uncle.

"Well," I said, "it's cold outside."

I looked down at my shiny black shoes and well creased new trousers and said, "I don't know when I shall wear my birthday suit again."

"When you next have a bath," said Jean.

We all laughed.

I was glad to go to my bedroom; my family had shared the experience, but didn't know how to express it. They were not into showing emotion. However, I was buzzing. Everything that had happened, every sound, every experience was in my head going round and round. I tried to recall as much as I could. The faces of some of the players who looked at me, first bewildered and then with absolute concentration as they waited for my signal to bring them in. Eventually I saw trust which was very reassuring to me. I relished every memory and tried to relive as much as possible. Best was the total interaction between piano and orchestra. Had I really done that? It seemed now like a dream. I lay there for what seemed like hours.

The music went on and on in my head till I fell asleep. It was school on Monday and I was a little apprehensive, what would my friends say, let alone the sixth formers from the orchestra?

As expected, when I parked my bike in the sheds, I turned to find a small crowd. Dennis was there, as was Mike, Bunny and three others. They were simply the advance guard as I found later.

"What's all these rumours going round about you conducting the school orchestra, with the Canon playing?"

They all said pretty much the same version all at once, so it was a cacophony of noise. I raised both hands as if in surrender.

"Guilty as charged," I said.

"Strewth, you kept that close to your chest," Dennis said, with a certain accusation in his voice.

"Sorry, Dennis," I replied, "but sworn to secrecy by the Canon."

Dennis said, "Even from me?"

I felt guilty. "Actually, the time to let you into the secret never came."

He was slightly mollified, I hoped. The others were not so easily satisfied.

"How the devil did you do it?" was said more than once.

By now the group had swollen to ten or more.

"Well, it seems I can remember the scores of music and the Canon wanted to demonstrate it."

"Didn't you take a huge risk?" said Mike.

"He had tested me more than once," I told him.

"But the programme said 'Guest Conductor'. I've seen a copy," said Bunny. "That means the orchestra didn't know either."

"True," I said.

"What the devil did they think when you turned up on the stage?"

"I'm not sure," I said, "but that didn't mean they didn't play as they were supposed to."

At this moment the bell rang and we all went our ways. I knew they hadn't finished with me, but at break the questions were less accusing and more to do with how I kept my nerve. During the lunch hour I was approached by the sixth former who had played trumpet so well. I was about to tell him how impressed I was when he said, "I don't know what Rust was playing at on Saturday, but I was not impressed by an Oik like you trying to take over our orchestra. You seemed to keep time, but my entry was from the music not because you pointed at me."

"Well," I said, "all of the entries must have been despite me because they were all on time. Despite what you have said, I thought your playing was brilliant, even though you probably don't care for my opinion."

He grunted and walked away. Well, I thought, you can't win them all.

I was a seven-day wonder as people say and we were back to normal soon.

The Canon did call me to his room as was expected on the following day when things were a little quieter.

"Well," he said, my usual conversation starter, "what do you think now that you have time to absorb it all?"

"Well, Sir, I really enjoyed it though I doubt I will ever do such a thing again."

"Probably not," he said, "though that is possibly regrettable. You could easily have had a musical career and I'm beginning to think it's not too late."

He looked hard at me to see my reaction. I blushed slightly, pleased with his faith in my strange ability.

I replied thoughtfully, "Thank you for your belief in me, but I really think that my pathway has been laid out."

"You mean this geology and such?" he said.

"Not quite that," I replied "I'm really hoping to study anthropology, a new science."

This new word had recently appeared in my mind and I had some trouble finding the definition, but when I had, I knew that this was something I wanted to explore. "The other subjects I mentioned in our recent meeting are merely the means to this end. I will have to qualify in some before I can even start my chosen career."

"Well," he said, "I stand corrected, Freddie, you have it all planned and well thought out. Nevertheless, I enjoyed playing on Saturday, possibly more than you enjoyed your performance. By the way, how did it go down with your friends?"

"They were astonished," I said, "and generally bewildered, but one of the sixth formers called me an oik, and hinted I should leave his orchestra alone."

To my surprise the Canon roared with laughter.

He said, "You probably don't realise, but many of the sixth formers came into this school before the 1945 Education Act when it was a fee-paying public school. Many of them never quite got over the fact that talented boys from other schools could come here, so if I were you, I would ignore his comment."

"I did, Sir" I said, "but I still told him he played brilliantly."

"Ah," said the Canon "I think I know who you are talking about; it makes sense. I can tell you the feedback from most of the orchestra was very positive, once they got over their initial shock."

"By the way," he said looking again at me directly, "Define anthro..."

"Anthropology," I said.

"Ah yes, not something I have come across."

"I'm not surprised," I said, "work has been going on for many years, but only recently has it been given a name and the various findings are beginning to be collated."

"You do use some very technical words," the Canon said. "So, what does it study?"

"The development of the human race via tools, bones and so on and the various humans who existed before our current one, that is Homo sapiens, 'man the wise' I think it means, though I'm not sure I agree completely. The name was only used for the first time in 1939," I told him.

"Again, you astonish me, Freddie. I'm sure that whatever you do, you will have a brilliant career and we in this school will do all in our power to assist you achieve your aims."

"Thank you, Sir," I said, feeling considerable gratitude. "And by the way I really enjoyed your performance as I'm sure everyone else did; it was really virtuoso."

"Thank you, Freddie, the whole plot allowed me to do something that I have not done in public for many years."

With this our meeting broke up and I could look forward to my next adventure. Actually, there were none that were embarrassing.

Anthony Winnall

CHAPTER 9

The hostel trip came and went and it was very enjoyable with about 15 of us including a boy in the lower 6th who was doing art A level. He wasn't a prefect, so he was no threat to us. Mr Viner stayed with his parents some way away, so we were left to our own devices.

We mostly walked everywhere. Each morning after the warden had given us our chores, 'Charlie' would arrive at the hostel in his Austin 7 and tell us where to meet. We walked in our cadet boots and school macs and, using 1inch Ordnance Survey maps, we would find footpaths across the hills to a village with the church he had chosen for us. At night in our dormitory, which fortunately had only our party in it, we were surprisingly well behaved. Well, perhaps reasonably well behaved, we were 15 and 16 after all. We made sure the warden of the hostel had no complaints and that we didn't disturb folk in the nearby rooms. Was this because we were intrinsically good? I don't think so for one minute. The discipline of the school had a long reach and we all decided we didn't want to embarrass Charlie who had chosen to give us this rare opportunity in his school holiday as well as ours.

One unusual experience was when on the edge of a path we came across a long barrow, a Neolithic burial place. It had an open entrance and we were able to explore it. I realised that this was part of my future. Had 'Brain' organised this as well for me? I had no idea. The close proximity of us all in the hostel did allow us all to see each other in a different light. When you're in a dorm with everyone in their pyjamas, it's a great leveller. That was another bonus to the trip.

I'm sure that this week did a lot to ensure we all passed art in the O level exams. They took place shortly after the next school holiday, a week off at Whit. We were given two weeks off school for revision. I spent most of my time in the back garden since it coincided with a rare summer heatwave.

Mike - I have sat next to Freddie in art since the first year. He has been a steady friend and we have had lots of laughs. Art is possibly the only subject where this is possible. Charlie is such a good teacher. I'm good at art. Possibly one of the best in the class, though I have to admit I do put birds into my work whatever Charlie says we are to illustrate. He is remarkably tolerant.

Freddie is obsessed with cacti and it's not so easy for him to put them in, but he somehow manages it. It is a sort of bonding thing that we have this quirk.

On the hostel trip, I had the opportunity to see some new birds. The others weren't interested I know. I didn't care. I spend a lot of time at weekends on my own in the places I know are good for spotting. On the trip, I was in a group of about six of us. We listened to Charlie's orders each morning, got our packed lunches and set off to the next church. I was generally at the back of the group because the lads in front would often disturb a bird and it would fly up and I could get a good view.

I was interested in the churches and everything we were told which would help in the exams which were coming up soon after we returned, but the new birds were great and I loved the trip.

I should mention that Freddie showed a side of himself which was new. In class he was fairly quiet, talking only to me or Brian on his other side in art lessons. I took this for granted. On this trip I saw a different Freddie. All right, I knew he was doing very well in most lessons, especially English, and had come on a lot in the last few terms. I had also heard some rumours that he seemed to know the future. I took no notice of this nonsense. But now he always seemed to be the group leader. Map in hand he led the way, always at the front and we never had to think about where we were going. We had all been trained in map reading both in geography and in Cadets, but that was theory, this was different. Freddie seemed to have an unerring sense of direction and we as a group always got to the next village and church on time and often ahead of the other two groups. We let him get on with it. It did puzzle me because it was a rather more confident Freddie than I had seen till then.

Freddie - Well, I'm not going to bore you with too many details, so I will give you a summary. I and all of my friends had respectable results. Dennis had a placement with a firm of accountants to work his way up via annual exams.

Bunny went to work as a trainee public health inspector, as he intended. In the quad he was often telling us the grim details of 'botulism', a form of food poisoning. Like me, he was venturing into a field outside the experience of our quaint old-fashioned school.

Mike had a place at the local art college.

Terry entered the 6th form, one of very few. Somehow, I knew he would not stay long and that he was going to leave the country.

The end of term was something of an anticlimax. We were told that after finishing exams there was no need to go back to school till results day, unless of course we were heading for the 6th form. This only applied to one of my friends; most had found their opportunities largely by their own efforts, I think.

I found a local college, designed for students of all ages, which did A level courses as well as technical courses. They were extremely helpful and I, now 16, felt able to organise courses without parental help. So, I launched into the career 'Brain' had in mind for me.

I think it was during this introduction to the freedom of college life that I realised what the music was all about. It had given me confidence, especially the orchestral experience. After that, I knew I could look the world in the eye and speak to anyone on adult terms. Thanks 'Brain'.

The college lecturer in biology suggested I need not do O level, but start A level which I would do over two years. I carried on with two other of my main subjects and to my astonishment found I could do A level geology in one year by doing an afternoon and an evening session, year one and year two respectively.

Again, not to bore you, it meant I could, after two years at the age of 18, apply to university. With 4 A levels and a handful of O levels I had a good choice. I chose a new university in north Staffordshire where I was accepted on interview and would spend four years and it was a requirement to graduate in two subjects.

During this time my accommodation was in what was a former RAF hut on the campus. This had rooms for 6 students with a bathroom and kitchen. I was happy there and I took my record player with me. This meant many a musical evening with like-minded friends and a great increase in repertoire and 'Brain' wasn't really needed.

I'm not sure how I became aware that at this stage that I was on my own and 'Brain' was no longer there, but it happened. It was a bit of a shock when it finally dawned on me, but the work had been done apparently. I coped with the work and greatly enjoyed it. There was no anthropology as yet. My geology professor said he knew of no university offering this yet, but with my two degree subjects I was as well prepared as anyone.

He knew I was specialising in palaeontology and suggested an M.Sc. specialising in the most recent geological periods where Hominid specimens were to be found, albeit mostly in far off places. He indicated I would be well advised to offer to help with 'digs' in Kenya and such places. This was what I did and it all worked out, as it seemed to have been planned all those years ago.

From time to time, I would try to work out what had happened to me. I had thought it was impossible to communicate with anyone in the future "because the future hadn't happened". But here I was now into my future looking back on young Freddie, and I realised I was looking at what had happened and both existed, though in different times. It was a breakthrough. So 'Brain' was my future. He, or rather me, had been very helpful, but the communication had stopped. As time went on, I thought about this enigma less and less. My career awaited me and the way had been smoothed.

CHAPTER 10

Professor Freddie Windsor CBE, FRS, sat on the stage in Big School. He looked at the faces staring at him. He had just finished the prize-giving and as the guest of honour had given the usual congratulatory speech. Prior to this, the current Head, the first female Head in over 500 years, of this now co-educational school, had outlined his distinguished career, giving great prominence to the part the school had played in opening up new opportunities.

Professor Freddie Windsor, yes, he had still kept the same name, smiled to himself as he listened to the talk, knowing how limited and narrow the curriculum was in those days, adequate no doubt for civil servants and government ministers, not much use for any other career, in fact, completely useless for the career he himself had pursued. It was the first time he had been back to the school since 1954. He realised he was wearing the same black bow tie which the Canon had tied for him as a boy all those years ago on the night of the concert.

Yes, he had forged new pathways in the understanding of the past. The development of human species and in more recent times the spread of Homo Sapiens throughout the world based on unusual evidence, a career which had rewarded him with many honours. It was, he thought, exactly the career I described to my dad, except I called it archaeology because at that time I didn't know about anthropology. His parents had lived to see some of it, he was pleased to recollect.

He looked back on his life as he watched the audience whilst a Governor gave a vote of thanks. He had never revealed to anyone how a few years ago his other experiments had led him to the realisation that he could communicate telepathically with his younger self and thus helped him breakout of the blind alley into which he had fallen at the beginning of his younger school life.

He remembered how young Freddie had eventually worked out that it was his future self that was helping him and that 'Brain' was not some mystery being. He regretted that communication was entirely one way. After all, the past existed and the future in theory was as yet unwritten. That was the dilemma which had bewildered young Freddie and himself. But eventually he had decided that young Freddie was ready to go his own way, once he had ensured that college pathways would be open to Freddie.

He did not regret flooding Freddie with a knowledge and love of music. He had always had it. But then he had given it to himself. He could never grapple with the philosophical dilemma this caused. What did this mean to 'past' and 'future', let alone present existence? Also, it wasn't really telepathy because he was only talking or more accurately thinking to himself. He was too old to explore these ideas now. The year was 2020 and retired Professor Freddie now aged 82 was about to leave the stage to retreat to the Head's study with other guests. He noted that none were from his era. Not a surprise, such folks needed to be in their prime, not an Emeritus Professor like himself. He did know one or two survivors from his school years. Dennis was still a longstanding friend, now of course retired from a position as company secretary of a large firm. Others too came to mind and he remembered the prophecy concerning Terry. Five years earlier he had made contact with Terry in New Zealand via Facebook and they had regular contact via email. He hadn't reminded Terry of his foresight. It had happened though. He realised that this recent connection must have somehow reached Freddie many years ago.

His own time was limited. He had realised that all his communications with his younger self lay between Freddie's third year in school and when he had stopped the communication when Freddie was in the second year of his degree course. At this point Freddie could stand on his own feet.

As he rose to his feet, he could not fail to remember the last time he had stood on this stage. A concert, a piece chosen by himself, and an innocent orchestra who didn't know what to expect. He was just short of his sixteenth birthday when this had happened. The Canon had played brilliantly and the orchestra had rehearsed hard and not let him down. He thought back to the entry of various sections, all had come in on time according to his direction. It had been an amazing experience which had made him something of a phenomenon in his last few weeks at school. Fortunately, the impending O levels and the two weeks study leave which preceded them had helped the majority to lose interest. Thus, he had departed to a college which could assist his future needs.

As Professor Freddie walked down the central aisle with the Head followed by the other dignitaries, he contemplated the school's changes which he had noted in an earlier tour. No longer could he accuse it of being behind in the sciences. In fact, the range of subjects had amazed him. There was an actual theatre for studies and performances, the Art Gallery was named after his old favourite teacher; this had particularly pleased him. Of course, the school was again fee paying, hence the vast improvements, but it was offering bursaries to less well off pupils.

I wonder if I would have been good enough to earn one of those as a 'late developer', he chuckled to himself.

He thought back to the year 1958 when he had stopped communicating with his younger self. He found it hard to believe it had happened and he had never been able to explain it, though it had seemed so easy at the time. His busy life had occupied him naturally, but once in his 50s he had tried to contact younger Freddie. It was not successful. Maybe the younger Freddie had fought back and resisted the thought.

The Head could not understand why Professor Freddie was so cheerful and constantly smiling. Freddie laughed inside and the chuckle broke out.

The End

SUGGESTIONS FOR  S

1. **THE ROOM** Discourage people from sit[...] – all need to be equally involved.

2. **HOSPITALITY** Tea or coffee on arrival [...]g. Perhaps at the end too, to encourage p[...]s might be more ambitious, taking it in turns to bring a dessert to start the evening (even in Lent, hospitality is OK!) with coffee at the end.

3. **THE START** If group members don't know each other well, some kind of 'icebreaker' might be helpful. For example, you might invite people to share something quite secular (where they grew up, holidays, hobbies, etc.). Place a time limit on this exercise.

4. **PREPARING THE GROUP** Take the group into your confidence, e.g. 'I've never done this before', or 'I've led lots of groups and each one has contained surprises'. Sharing vulnerability encourages all members to see the success of the group as their responsibility. Ask those who know that they talk easily to ration their contributions, and encourage the reticent to speak at least once or twice – however briefly. Explain that there are no 'right' answers and that among friends it is fine to say things that you are not sure about – to express half-formed ideas. However, if individuals choose to say nothing, that's all right too.

5. **THE MATERIAL** Encourage members to read each session *before* the meeting. It helps enormously if each group member has their own personal copy of this booklet (so the price is reduced either when multiple copies are ordered or if you order online). *There is no need to consider all the questions.* A lively exchange of views is what matters, so be selective. You can always spread a session over two or more meetings if you run out of time!

   For some questions you might start with a few minutes' silence to make jottings. Or you might ask members to talk in sub-groups of two or three, before sharing with the whole group.

6. **PREPARATION** Decide beforehand whether to distribute (or ask people to bring) paper, pencils, etc. If possible, ask people in advance to read a Bible passage or lead in prayer, so that they can prepare.

7. **TIMING** Try to start on time and make sure you stick fairly closely to your stated finishing time.

8. **USING THE CD** There is no 'right' way! Some groups will play the 15-minute piece at the beginning of the session. Other groups do things differently – perhaps playing it at the end, or playing 7/8 minutes at the beginning and the rest halfway through the meeting. The track markers (on the CD and shown in the Transcript) will help you find any question put to the participants very easily, including the Closing Reflections, which you may wish to play (again) at the end of the session. Do whatever is best for you and your group.

SESSION 1

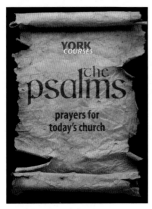

KNOW THAT THE LORD IS GOD

> Wonder is the basis of worship.
> *Thomas Carlyle*
>
> The most valuable thing the Psalms do for me is to express the same delight in God which made David dance.
> *C S Lewis*
>
> There is no such thing known in heaven as Sunday worship unless it is accompanied by Monday worship and Tuesday worship and so on.
> *A W Tozer, American pastor*

> To worship is to quicken the conscience by the holiness of God, to feed the mind with the truth of God, to purge the imagination by the beauty of God, to open the heart to the love of God, to devote the will to the purposes of God.
> *Archbishop William Temple*

Psalm 100

> Different translations of the psalms use different verse numbers. So we suggest you use the Common Worship version set out in this course booklet.

This course explores five particular psalms. Each one addresses a profound human emotion. Each one gives us a text and a template for expressing these feelings before God. They also give us wisdom for navigating our way through the similar challenges and delights that we will encounter in life. When you don't know what to pray, when you are not sure how to make sense of a situation or an emotion, when anger is suppressed or joy restrained, the psalms are there, providing words for you to inhabit. The psalms are a library of praise and petition for us to recite and build our prayers upon. They are the 'Prayer Book' of the Bible.

Emotions are fuel for prayer

When we have troubles or when we are joyful, there is nothing more natural than to cry out to God. But often we don't seem to have the words to say, or we feel too timid to tell it as it is. The gift of the psalms is one of the ways God helps us. He gives us words for our prayer and praise. Martin Luther once complained that many people's prayers seemed to him to be 'trifling little devotions'. He went on: *'There is none of the sap, the strength, the fervour and the fire that I find in the Psalms.'*

I hope this course shapes your prayer. I hope this course ignites you.

Psalm 100

1 *O be joyful in the Lord, all the earth;*
   serve the Lord with gladness
   and come before his presence with a song.

2 *Know that the Lord is God;*
   it is he that has made us and we are his;
   we are his people and the sheep of his pasture.

3 *Enter his gates with thanksgiving*
   and his courts with praise;
   give thanks to him and bless his name.

4 *For the Lord is gracious; his steadfast love is everlasting,*
   and his faithfulness endures from generation to
   generation.

A Sunday School teacher once commented to me that whereas adults' prayers usually began with the word *'please'*, children's prayers usually began with the words *'thank you.'* It is a wry and painfully accurate observation. When we adults come to God, it is often because we want something. Even on those occasions when we are not just asking for things for ourselves, we often have a wish list of the things in the world God really ought to be sorting out if he were a half-decent sort of God. Of course, we secretly believe we could do a much better job, and can't quite understand why the God we've got is so slow off the mark!

But children say thank you. Their prayers begin with a litany of gratitude for the people and things that have brought them comfort and joy. From this heart of thanksgiving other good things follow: appreciation for what is, and delight in those who provide them.

Thanksgiving – seeing life as God's gift

Thanksgiving is the seedbed of praise and adoration. The psalms overflow with all three. Psalm 136 is one long list of 'thank yous'. Psalm 18 is a beautiful and heartfelt song of adoration and thanksgiving. And Psalm 150, the last in the book of Psalms, is just one short, sharp burst of praise.

Psalm 100, on which we are focussing in this session, is also a psalm of joyful praise. We are invited to come before God's presence *'with a song'* and to enter his courts *'with praise'*.

But all this praising can be problematic. Our detractors are not slow to point out that in their estimation, any God who needs praising all the time must either be deeply insecure, or vain beyond measure.

The real reason leads us somewhere else. The influential Trappist monk Thomas Merton observed that, *'if we have no real interest in praising God it shows that we have never realised who He is.'*

To praise God is to acknowledge and learn who God is. God is the maker and creator of all things. It is not just that God cares for us and has an interest in us (though he does): God is the source and ground of our being, and without God there is nothing. *'Know that the Lord is God,'* says the psalmist, *'It is he that has made us and we are his …'*

3

Therefore to thank God for the gift of each day, each meal, each breath, is simply to acknowledge the reality of our relationship: God the creator, we the created. God has been faithful to us: he has raised up a people to know him and serve him. This is another of the themes of Psalm 100: *'The Lord is gracious ... his faithfulness endures from generation to generation.'* To praise God is to acknowledge the truth about ourselves: that we are dependent, not self-sufficient.

A relationship of love

As Christians we believe that this story of God's faithfulness reaches its fulfilment in Jesus. By expressing our love for God and thanking him for:

- the creation of the world and our creation
- the redemption he has won for us in Christ
- his faithfulness to us

we grow in the understanding of our faith – and our God.

The Christian faith is not a list of things for us to believe in, nor just a record of God's achievements, but rather *the creation of a relationship of love* whereby we enjoy communion with God. Thus, to love and adore God is to enter most deeply into the truth of the Christian faith that *'God is love, and those who abide in love, abide in God'.* (1 John 4.16.) Our relationship with God is the source of our joy.

Just as human relationships are nurtured and sustained by thanksgiving, adoration and praise, so it is with our relationship with God. When my wife says she loves me, it is a declaration of the deepest truth of our relationship and all that has flowed from it, and all the commitment, heartache and hard work that has gone into it. And if I just say 'ditto' in return, taking that love for granted, then I fail to acknowledge or express either my responsibility or my joy. But when I say the words, when I reply, 'I love you', I not only express the true nature of our relationship, however hard it may have been at times, I expand my capacity for loving.

But we are talking about loving God, and his great initiative of love in the creation of the world, and in the death and resurrection of his Son. So my praise of God not only expands my love for God, but my ability to love the world and to inhabit it with a thankful heart.

The psalms encourage us to be exuberant in our praise. Overflow with love! Bang the drum! Blast the trumpet! Sing of God's love and God's love will be with you.

Antidote to cynicism

The psalms are an education in praise. In a world which can be cynical and self-obsessed, and can take delight in the downfall of others, to pray these psalms of joyful thanksgiving is to learn how to be thankful and how to build a relationship with God the right way round. As St Augustine put it: 'God wants to be loved not in order that He may get something out of it, but in order that those who love Him may receive an eternal reward. And this reward is God Himself, whom they love.' Therefore …

'let everything that has breath praise the Lord!'
(Psalm 150.6.)

There is an ancient tradition of reading the psalms antiphonally. So, to start your discussion, you might like to read aloud the psalm for this session We suggest that the leader reads out the lines in colour and that the group members speak the lines in black.

The structure of many psalms lends itself to this way of reading, since in most of them one line builds on the theme of the previous line.

Psalm 120.1 for example:-

When I was in trouble I called to the Lord;
I called to the Lord and he answered me.

After the reading allow a minute for silent reflection. Which word, phrase, thought or overall impression strikes you on this first reading? What would you give as the title for this Psalm?

QUESTIONS FOR GROUPS
BIBLE READING: PSALM 100 – see p. 2

Some groups will address all the questions. That's fine. Others may prefer to select just a few and spend longer on each. That's fine, too. Horses for (York) Courses!

Please see the suggestion in the box at the bottom of p. 5 about reading the Psalm together.

1. **Psalm 100** is joyful. Do your faith and worship bring you joy? Or do you sometimes feel that worship is a duty to be performed? Do you agree with Milton Jones' words in the box on p. 5? (Our distinguished CD participants discuss this on track 3 of the course CD/transcript.)

2. **Read John 4.24.** Many older churchgoers recall singing or saying psalms every week – no longer the case in many churches. Have we lost something precious, as Bishop Stephen believes, or are most services too wordy and too long already? What do you do if church worship is hard-going and your concentration wanders?

3. **Read Romans 12.1.** A young child asks why you go to church, and you tell him that you go to worship God. The child replies, 'What is worship?' How would you reply? (Track 4 of the course CD/transcript addresses this.)

4. His sceptical teenage sister chips in, 'Yeah, you sing hymns and stuff and that makes you feel better when you get on with your own comfortable little life.' Your response please. (Track 5 of the course CD/transcript.)

5. Bishop Stephen Cottrell suggests that the words of the psalms give us a template for our prayer, our praise – and our deep emotions. They give us words we might otherwise feel too timid to say. Do you have a favourite psalm? You might select and read aloud a verse or two that express your own longings and prayers?

6. **Read Colossians 3.22 and the box about the 'Sock Lady' on p. 4.** Psalm 100.1 says 'Serve the Lord with gladness.' How can/do/should we 'serve the Lord'? And if it involves long hours or boring chores, how can we do it 'with gladness'?

7. **Read A W Tozer's words in the box on p. 2.** On track 5 Rose Hudson-Wilkin says, 'If our worship does not connect with our everyday lives then we are probably barking up the wrong tree.' How does Sunday morning connect with Monday morning in your life?

8. Think of a recent problem in your life: how did worship, the Bible (especially the psalms) and/or your faith in God help you?

9. **Read Mark 8.34.** On track 6 John Bell says, 'Discipleship isn't a grudge thing. So we serve the Lord with gladness when we enjoy being disciples with a sense of privilege and anticipation.' Yes, but … most of us, some of the time, are reluctant disciples (e.g. a Christian teenager or soldier might be mocked; or our discipleship might take us into some unpleasant/difficult situations). Do you, like John Bell, enjoy being a disciple? Describe the last time you experienced that 'sense of privilege and anticipation' he mentions.

10. **Re-read Psalm 100.4 and Vince Neil's words in the box on p. 4.** On track 7 John Bell says: 'bad things happen to good people. And faith is not an insurance policy against that.' How do all these varying statements relate to each other – and to your own experience?

11. **Read Ephesians 5.19.** Rose sings hymns as she moves about (track 4) – even in the House of Commons! While Fr Timothy thinks that 'happy-clappy joy often does not endure' (track 6). Horses for courses, maybe? Perhaps different approaches work for different 'personality types'? What do you think?

12. Has there been a time recently when you have felt joyful and grateful, like the psalmist? What triggered this? It might be an encouragement if you would share this with your group. Did you just enjoy the experience, or – like the psalmist – did you consciously thank God for it?

SESSION 2

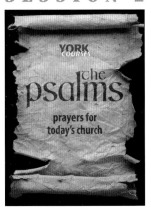

YORK COURSES

the psalms
prayers for today's church

OUT OF THE DEPTHS HAVE I CRIED

Psalm 130

I especially love the psalms because they give voice to my own deepest feelings and aspirations before God. Even more than this, they give me words and phrases that express feelings and aspirations that might otherwise remain unexpressed. At the same time they give permission for my joy to be exuberant, my frustration to be uninhibited, and my anger to be released.

There is something about the psalms that means whatever you are feeling about almost any given situation, there is a psalm that will match it and trump it. So if you are feeling joyful, there is a psalm that is more joyful than you. If you are feeling desperate, there is a psalm that is more desperate than you. If you are feeling alienated or alone, there is a psalm that is more isolated than you – witness the words of Christ from the cross: *'My God, my God, why have you forsaken me?'* (Psalm 22.1.)

This is not the false comfort that tells us not to worry because someone somewhere is worse off than you. It is the astonishing scaling of heights and plumbing of depths whereby the psalms express and expand every possible sentiment and desire about life lived in community with God. As such the psalms live on. They fire the imagination; they fuel our praise; they provide text and narrative when there is nothing else to say. They encourage us to be real with God – and with ourselves.

Psalm 130

1 *Out of the depths have I cried to you, O Lord;*
Lord, hear my voice;
let your ears consider well the voice of my supplication.

2 *If you, Lord, were to mark what is done amiss,*
O Lord, who could stand?

3 *But there is forgiveness with you,*
so that you shall be feared.

4 *I wait for the Lord; my soul waits for him;*
in his word is my hope.

5 *My soul waits for the Lord,*
more than the night watch for the morning,
more than the night watch for the morning.

6 *O Israel, wait for the Lord,*
for with the Lord there is mercy;

7 *With him is plenteous redemption*
and he shall redeem Israel from all their sins.

> How wonderful it is that nobody need wait a single moment before starting to improve the world!
>
> *Anne Frank*

> I was never good at being patient, but I've learned to trust God, his provision and his timing. It's difficult for me to see the changes, but I'm told that I'm calmer now, and much more reliable.
>
> *Lynne Bradley, singer, writer and cancer survivor*

> God will not look you over for medals, degrees or diplomas but for scars.
>
> *Elbert Hubbard, writer*

'There's a wideness in God's mercy'

The psalms are wonderfully realistic about our relationship with God. *'If you, Lord, were to mark what is done amiss, O Lord, who could stand?'* If God were to weigh us in the scales, measuring our goodness, we would all be lost.

Compared with God's righteousness, our own attitudes, behaviour and inclinations fall woefully short of what they should be. *'I have been wicked even from my birth, a sinner when my mother conceived me,'* says Psalm 51.5. This one verse brilliantly encapsulates the biblical view: we have what might be called an inbuilt disposition to get it wrong, to act selfishly and to chase after what we know to be wrong. Who hasn't lain awake at night raking over the events of the day – wishing we had acted differently, or said something other than we did? We fall short of our own standards, let alone the standards of God.

The Bible tells us that God's very nature is of loving kindness and mercy. *'With you there is forgiveness,'* says the psalmist. God longs to restore us to a right relationship, by blotting out our sins and by leading us in the ways of his goodness. So when Jesus is questioned about the company he keeps, he replies, *'Those who are well have no need of a physician, but those who are sick. Go and learn what this means, "I desire mercy, not sacrifice." For I have come to call not the righteous but sinners.'* (Matthew 9.12-13.)

This is echoed in Psalm 51.16-17: *'You desire no sacrifice, else I would give it,'* but *'the sacrifice of God is a broken spirit, a broken and contrite heart, O God, you will not despise'.*

Psalm 130 ends with a promise:

> *O Israel, wait for the Lord,*
> *for with the Lord there is mercy;*
> *With him is plenteous redemption*
> *and he shall redeem Israel from all their sins.*

This redemption is what we have seen and received in Jesus. Through Jesus' death and resurrection a right relationship with God is restored.

Penitence and forgiveness

In order to receive this reconciliation we must enter by the door of penitence. Praying the psalms enables this to happen. The psalms help us to be realistic about

ourselves. They nurture a spirit of contrition, whereby we
know our need of God.

Then I acknowledged my sin to you
and my iniquity I did not hide.
I said, 'I will confess my transgressions to the Lord,'
and you forgave the guilt of my sin. (Psalm 32.5)

We too need to confess our sins – and the psalms give us
the words to do this. We come to the Lord with humble
hearts, acknowledging our wickedness and failure. Psalm
51 is perhaps the best known of the penitential psalms. It
begins with these words:

Have mercy on me, O God, in your great goodness;
according to the abundance of your compassion
blot out my offences.

Wash me thoroughly from my wickedness
and cleanse me from my sin.

For I acknowledge my faults
and my sin is ever before me.

This penitence is not grovelling, because the psalms
usually lead us on to praise and thanksgiving. Psalm 32
ends: *'Be glad you righteous, and rejoice in the Lord, shout
for joy, all who are true of heart.'*

Penitence opens us up to amendment of life. Although
we will never arrive at a point where we no longer need
to confess our sins, facing up to them enables us to resist
temptation and live lives of greater transparency and
purpose. *'Teach me to do what pleases you,'* pleads Psalm
143; *'Let your kindly spirit lead me on a level path.'* While
Psalm 51 begs, *'Make me a clean heart'*.

Why do the wicked prosper?

Equally, these penitential psalms – and quite a few
others – do not shirk from a more troublesome issue:
why is it that the wicked prosper, yet those who are
penitent seem to carry on suffering? Many of the
psalms grapple with this, and point towards the
ultimate judgement of God. In fact the whole of Psalm
37 addresses this question, exhorting us to *'fret not
because of evildoers'*. And Psalm 73 despairs at the
apparent prosperity of the wicked, until the psalmist
enters the Temple to worship God and sees how there
will be a reckoning.

Despite the belief in God's vindication, the psalms also express an all too human desire for revenge, as the psalmist calls down God's wrath upon the enemy. Let me give you just one grisly example, which comes towards the end of the otherwise sublimely beautiful Psalm 139:

O that you would slay the wicked, O God,
that the bloodthirsty might depart from me!

They speak against you with wicked intent;
your enemies take up your name for evil.

Do I not oppose those, O Lord, who oppose you?
Do I not abhor those who rise up against you?

I hate them with a perfect hatred;
they have become my own enemies also.

Use or discard?

How do we pray words like these? After all, is not our own behaviour wicked? Isn't this what God calls us to acknowledge? Does God really wish to slay us as well? Or are these curses merely a primitive remnant from an earlier period of religious development?

Some individuals and churches solve the conundrum by simply omitting the offending verses, but this seems to me to be a cheat. For the urge for vengeance can stir within all of us. To dare to say these words within the larger context of penitence and praise enables us to acknowledge the hatreds that can exist within us too.

Walter Brueggemann puts it like this: *'When we know ourselves as well as the Psalter knows us, we recognise that we are creatures who wish for vengeance and retaliation.'* Therefore by owning the reality of these dark forces and motivations we are better able to receive and live by the devastating truths that Jesus brings us: *'For you have heard that it was said, "You shall love your neighbour and hate your enemy." But I say to you, Love your enemies and pray for those who persecute you, so that you may be children of your Father in heaven; for he makes his sun rise on the evil and on the good, and sends rain on the righteous and on the unrighteous.'* (Matthew 5.43-45.)

QUESTIONS FOR GROUPS

BIBLE READING: PSALM 130 – see p. 7

Some groups will address all the questions. That's fine. Others may prefer to select just a few and spend longer on each. That's fine, too. Horses for (York) Courses!

Please see the suggestion in the box at the bottom of p. 5 about reading the Psalm together.

1. 'All things come to him who waits.' Do they? How does this fit with our must-have-it-now society? Is patience still a virtue?

2. **Re-read Psalm 130.4.** Are you a patient person in your daily life? More than once in this psalm we read about waiting for the Lord. What does it mean to 'wait for the Lord'? Does waiting become easier or harder with the passing years? (The participants discuss this on track 9 of the CD/transcript.)

3. **Read Matthew 21.12-13 and Romans 12.21.** Bishop Stephen writes that the Psalms 'give permission for my joy to be exuberant, my frustration to be uninhibited, and my anger to be released.' Joy and frustration, yes, but what place – if any – does anger have in the Christian life?

4. **Read 1 Corinthians 13.4-7.** On track 11 Rose comments amusingly on: 'love does not keep a record of wrongs'. Most of us struggle with this sometimes. Do you? Can you give an example from your own life?

5. **Read the box at the foot of p. 23.** Psalm 130.2 tells us that God does not keep a record of sins. We tend to turn this on its head – thinking that God keeps a record of all the good things we do. Tributes at funerals often contribute to the belief that if we gather more good points than negative points throughout our lives we secure salvation. How can we shift the emphasis from 'record-keeping' to relying on God's grace and forgiveness, as expressed in verses 2 and 3?

6. **Read Psalm 51.6 and the C S Lewis box on p. 8.** 'I have been wicked even from my birth, a sinner when my mother conceived me'. The Authorised Version might appear to suggest that sex is wrong: 'in sin did my mother conceive me.' On p. 8 Bishop Stephen clarifies this: 'This one verse brilliantly encapsulates the biblical view: we have what you might call an inbuilt disposition to get it wrong.' Many people, including some churchgoers, are unhappy with this stress on sin and being a sinner. What about you? Is it the Church or the press who are hung up on sex?

7. On track 12 Fr Timothy says, 'It's a thoroughly dangerous thing to get involved with God, because he might ask you to do extraordinary things. Turn your life upside-down.' Have you experience of this in your own life – or seen it/read about it in someone else's?

8. **Psalm 130.3** is puzzling. It speaks of God's grace and mercy shown in forgiveness. But instead of saying, 'so that you [God] shall be *loved* or *trusted*' it says, *'feared'.* What do you understand by the words 'loving God', 'trusting God' and 'fearing God'? (Track 12 might help.)

9. **Read 2 Corinthians 5.16-19.** 'Through Jesus' death and resurrection a right relationship with God is restored,' writes Bishop Stephen on p. 8. What do you understand by this?

10. **Read Ephesians 4.26 and theologian Walter Brueggemann's words on p. 10.** He says, 'we are creatures who wish for vengeance and retaliation.' Do you think he's right?

11. On p. 9 Bishop Stephen writes, 'The psalms help us to be realistic about ourselves. They nurture a spirit of contrition, whereby we know our need of God … In order to receive reconciliation we must enter by the door of penitence. Praying the psalms enables this to happen.' How can we open 'the door of penitence' to enter God's presence? What must we do? Are there any other doors into God's presence?

12. **Read Mark Ellen's words in the box on p. 9.** Do you believe we have (any) 'God-given rights'? If so, what are they?

SESSION 3

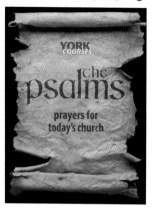

HOW LONG, O LORD?

We don't believe in a small God who is easy to fathom or who exists solely for our benefit. And yet when God doesn't do things the way we expect him to we can easily feel betrayed, leading us often to interpret the silence of God as the 'indifference of God'. The wrestling that this produces can be seen through the whole of scripture.

Krish Kandiah, theologian

The friend who can be silent with us in a moment of despair or confusion, who can stay with us in an hour of grief and bereavement, who can tolerate not knowing… not healing, not curing… that is a friend who cares.

Henri Nouwen, Catholic priest

Psalm 13

In *Hamlet*, the Queen brings the news that Ophelia has drowned, saying that as she died, *'she chanted snatches of old tunes as one incapable of her own distress.'* I suppose this is meant as an insult – Ophelia can't even find her own words for her own grief! But I find it a comfort: within her there were words that she had learnt from old songs, sustaining her and enabling her to give voice to her distress.

This is exactly how the psalms work.

Just as Ophelia found comfort in words that others had written and sung, so did Jesus himself as he was dying on the cross. His cry of anguish, *'My God, my God, why have you forsaken me?'* (Mark 15. 34) is actually the opening line of Psalm 22. Jesus' final words, *'Father, into your hands I commit my spirit'* (Luke 23.46) are from Psalm 31. Even his words, *'I am thirsty'* (John 19.28) allude to the psalms (Psalms 22.15 and 69.21).

Jesus died with the words of the psalms on his lips and in his heart. The words that he had learned in his youth sustained him. Some of these psalms, especially Psalm 22 and Psalm 69, now come to us as profound meditations on the passion itself, illuminating deep truths about the nature and meaning of Christ's death on the cross.

Psalm 13

1 *How long will you forget me, O Lord; for ever?*
   How long will you hide your face from me?

2 *How long shall I have anguish in my soul*
   and grief in my heart, day after day?
   How long shall my enemy triumph over me?

3 *Look upon me and answer, O Lord my God;*
   lighten my eyes, lest I sleep in death;

4 *Lest my enemy say, 'I have prevailed against him,'*
   and my foes rejoice that I have fallen.

5 *But I put my trust in your steadfast love;*
   my heart will rejoice in your salvation.

6 *I will sing to the Lord,*
   for he has dealt so bountifully with me.

With its repeated cry of anguish, *'How long, O Lord?'* Psalm 13 exemplifies that other great feature of the psalms: *lamentation.* Here is someone who has waited on the Lord, and who has cried out to God from the depths; but God is silent. The experience is of God's absence. God's face is hidden. And Psalm 13 is by no means the hardest or the bleakest of the psalms. Sometimes it is God's terror and wrath that overpower us (Psalm 88.15-16).

When God goes missing

Some of us have experienced the dejection arising from the 'silence of God' as expressed in Psalm 13. Sometimes it is the events of life, its sorrows and its horrors that weigh us down. Sometimes it is illness or bereavement. Sometimes it is the gnawing emptiness of abandonment or forced solitude. Sometimes it is the apparent absence of God. All these expressions of desolation – even desertion – are voiced in the psalms with shocking and nerve-tingling clarity. The psalms never pull a punch.

Nor – though for many of us this is as much a cause for irritation as comfort – do the psalms offer any particular answers. They face up to the rasping pain of suffering with a sober honesty. They do not gloss over it with pious humbug. They do not merely say it is God's punishment (though sometimes they reckon it is). They do not avert the gaze to something else. What they do, even in Psalm 88, is to bring it before God. *The astonishing thing about these psalms of despair is that they are still directed to God, to the God who feels so absent and the God who, the psalmist feels, has rejected them.*

From despair to praise – the road less travelled

The ending of Psalm 13 is typical, as it moves from despair to praise, without either diminishing the reality of the pain, or offering praise as a panacea. The psalmist invites us to trust God, even when everything seems against us. Go even further, he says: rejoice in God's faithfulness; remember God's goodness. Gordon Mursell puts it like this: '*Praise, in prayers of lament, is not naïve optimism, but the defiant refusal to accept the seeming inevitability of what is happening, and the determined willingness to lift God's future into the present and to celebrate it even when there is no sign whatsoever of it coming to pass.*'

This is extraordinarily hard. But it is a theme we find throughout scripture. The prophet Habakkuk, mired in complete desolation – no fruit on the vine, no crops in the field, no sheep in the pen – still responds: *'I will rejoice in the Lord; I will exult in the God of my salvation'* (Habakkuk 3.17-18). The prophet looks forward to the ultimate victory and restoration that God promises.

And Jesus himself prays for those who nail him to the cross. He reaches out to those who are condemned with him and places his trust in God. His anguished cry, *'My God, my God, why have you forsaken me'* demonstrates his complete association with the sorrows and privations of the world. Yet Psalm 22, from which he quotes, doesn't just give voice to deep sorrow; it ends with jubilant praise expressing confidence in God:

'Praise the Lord, you that fear him ...
He has saved my life for himself ...
this shall be told of the Lord for generations to come.
They shall come and make known his salvation ...'

Casting our cares on God

It is exceedingly difficult to have faith in God when life is hard, and this must be acknowledged. Yet the experience of many Christians – and many Jews over the ages – is that at times of sorrow and despair it *is* possible to put your trust in God. It is possible to bring *everything*, even your lack of faith, to God.

The psalms encourage us to do this. They give us words when we don't have any of our own. This instinct for praise, even from the depths of desolation, is also a form of resistance. We will not let despair overtake us. We will not let misery and oppression have the last word. We will go on believing in the light, even when we are plunged into utter darkness.

We see this in Jesus. We see it in many other heroes of our faith: the martyrs who went to their death praising God.

Missionary Allen Gardiner kept a diary in 1850 when he and his six companions were slowly dying of starvation in inhospitable Tierra del Fuego. He wrote: 'Poor and weak as we are, our boat is a very Bethel to our souls, for we feel and know that God is here. Asleep or awake, I am, beyond the power of expression, happy.'

His words inspired Victorian England – including Charles Darwin, who celebrated the later success of the mission with the following words in a letter to the South American Missionary Society in 1870: 'The success of the Tierra del Fuego Mission is most wonderful, and charms me ... It is a grand success. I shall feel proud if your committee think fit to elect me an honorary member of your society.'

QUESTIONS FOR GROUPS

BIBLE READING: PSALM 13 – see p. 12

Some groups will address all the questions. That's fine. Others may prefer to select just a few and spend longer on each. That's fine, too. Horses for (York) Courses!

Please see the suggestion in the box at the bottom of p. 5 about reading the Psalm together.

1. Tough times for the psalmist. On track 19 of the CD/transcript Timothy says, 'I think it's very important that we pray for each other. And even sometimes with each other. That helps to keep us going in the tough moments.' Do you ever pray with your Christian friends – or anyone else – outside of church? When might you do this – or offer to do this? What holds you back, if you don't?

2. **Read Acts 16.9-10.** The Bible suggests that God speaks to us in many different ways: through dreams, prayer, a voice, a friend, a coincidence, a Bible verse … The psalmist laments, because he has waited on the Lord and cried out to God 'from the depths' but God seems to remain silent: 'the dark night of the soul'. Do you expect God to 'speak' to you? How does God do this – and how do you cope if he seems distant or absent?

3. **Read 1 Peter 5.7 and Job 19.25.** In tough times Fr Timothy hangs on to the 'beautiful' word 'abide' (track 18). What sees you through your dark times? Share any words of encouragement for those who might be feeling like that right now?

4. **Re-read Psalm 13.5-6** which expresses wonderful positive sentiments. Do the final verses of this psalm capture your own day-to-day experience? What do the key words 'trust' and 'salvation' mean to you? Can you say with the psalmist, 'I will sing to the *Lord, for he has dealt so bountifully with me.'*? (Rose does, on track 20!)

5. On track 23 of the CD John Bell, commenting on his mother's death after a cruel illness, observes that 'the life we are given is not a life that comes with guarantees.' Imagine your life without your faith. How would you cope? Who do you thank for your gift of faith?

6. This psalm swings between despair, hope and joy. Bishop Stephen loves the psalms because they appear to speak to every situation. Yet one Christian couple have given up using a psalm in their daily devotions, because there's too much whingeing and 'poor me'. Yet for centuries the Church has incorporated the psalms in its daily worship. (Four times a day Fr Timothy says a psalm or two.) Are the psalms a staple of your own devotional life?

7. Psalm 13 begins in despair and ends with trust and hope. Can you recall a time in your own life (or someone else's) when troubles gave way to new beginnings and hope? How big a part did your personal faith play in this?

8. **Read Romans 5.3-5 and Canon John Holmes' words in the box on p. 13.** The psalmist is open and honest about his mood swings! So we don't have to feel guilty when we struggle to be optimistic. Sometimes it can be a great act of faith simply to admit, 'It's not working' – in church life, family life, at work or elsewhere. That admission can open us to new possibilities, which are hidden as long as we pretend all is going well. Have you ever experienced, or heard of, such 'new dawns'?

9. Reflect on difficult times in your own life: what and/or who helped you most? What did you learn that has helped you to help others?

10. 10. **Read James 1.2-4 and the box about Jenny Agutter's family on p. 14.** A terrible experience for the bereaved parents – and a very tough assignment for the Catholic priest. What do you make of the priest's words? What might you say to bring comfort at such a time?

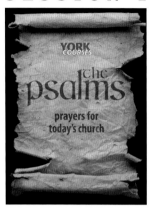

Psalm 23

The psalms have a very significant place in Christian liturgy and worship. But this is changing. While they are still said or sung in some churches, in many other congregations they have slipped out of use, and are becoming unfamiliar. Many churches no longer include a psalm in their regular services as a matter of course.

However, phrases and ideas from the psalms live on in our worship and sink into our memories. This might help to explain why we love them and know them – without necessarily realising that we love them and know them.

Psalm 23

YOU SPREAD A TABLE BEFORE ME

1 *The Lord is my shepherd;*
   therefore can I lack nothing.

2 *He makes me lie down in green pastures*
   and leads me beside still waters.

3 *He shall refresh my soul*
   and guide me in the paths of righteousness for his
   name's sake.

> Never be afraid to trust an unknown future to a known God.
>
> *Corrie ten Boom, writer*

4 *Though I walk through the valley of the shadow of*
   death, I will fear no evil;
   for you are with me;
   your rod and your staff, they comfort me.

5 *You spread a table before me*
   in the presence of those who trouble me;
   you have anointed my head with oil
   and my cup shall be full.

> The Church of England has warned that too many people are exhuming their dead relatives. The Ministry of Justice currently receives 25 exhumation requests a week; in parts of the country exhumation requests have risen sevenfold in five years. The Church says people expect to be able to bring their dead relatives along when they move house, not realising that the point of a Christian burial is to permanently 'entrust the person to God for resurrection'.
>
> *The Week, August 2015*

6 *Surely goodness and loving mercy shall follow me*
   all the days of my life,
   and I will dwell in the house of the Lord for ever.

The faithful God

Psalm 23 is not only the most famous of all the psalms; it is one of the best-known passages in the whole Bible – up there with the Beatitudes and 1 Corinthians 13. *The Lord is my Shepherd* appears consistently in anthologies of poetry. It is the basis for several very well known hymns. But what does it mean?

This is a psalm expressing great trust in God, even when life is hard and its trials unyielding. Many other psalms also respond to the iniquities and challenges of life with a similar graciousness and confidence, often speaking of God's actions in the past and using all sorts of images.

- **Psalm 121**, fearing the advance of enemies, affirms that the Lord will not let you stumble, and speaks of God as *'a keeper'* and as *'shade at your right hand'* so that *'the sun shall not strike you'*.

- **Psalm 105** retells key events in the salvation history of the people of Israel. The psalmist instructs the people and reminds them of God's faithfulness and saving love.

- **Psalm 84.10** speaks of the joy of worship, saying that a day in God's courts *'is better than a thousand elsewhere'*.

- **Psalm 119** (the longest psalm by far) is a meditation on the beauty of the law, and of God as the just and righteous law-giver.

- **Psalm 91.2** tells us that God is *'my refuge and my shelter,'* the one *'in whom I trust'*.

- **Psalm 77**, in a day of trouble, recalls God's mighty deeds and the ways that even the earth trembled before him.

The psalmist goes on to tell us that God led the people *'like a flock'* (Psalm 77.20). And it is this striking image of God as a shepherd to his people that sits at the heart of Psalm 23. This psalm still speaks powerfully to us today, even if most of us live in towns and cities and hardly ever see any sheep, let alone a shepherd. It is the image – so familiar in his day – taken up by Jesus when he describes himself as the *'Good Shepherd who lays down his life for the sheep'* (John 10.11).

God is with us in our fears

Psalm 23 speaks with a particular resonance to the fears and trepidations that all humanity encounters – including death itself. Some who read this booklet will, perhaps recently, have sat at the bedside of a loved one; kept vigil through the last circling hours of life; howled silently at our powerlessness; felt a chill dread at death's pitiless and unrelenting advance. Others, contemplating their own end, may have been gripped with fear. Death is indeed the darkest valley. The psalmist does not flinch from the reality of death, nor its inevitable approach. It is the path we will all tread.

Unsurprisingly, Psalm 23 is often read at funerals. It is a psalm of extraordinary comfort and hope.

But it is also often read at weddings, and sometimes at baptisms. At first this may seem a little odd, except that this most beautiful psalm also speaks of the joy and comfort that will be found *along the way*. It is a psalm about how we travel, not just where we are going. If the Lord is our shepherd, if he is the one in whom we put our trust, then we will lack nothing.

This does not mean life will be trouble-free. But it does mean that there is no need to be frightened of life. God is with you. There will be green pastures to rest in; there will be refreshing waters. For the sake of his name and his faithful covenant love, God will lead us and restore us. Anticipating the words of the Lord's Prayer itself, Psalm 23 tells us there will be no need to fear evil.

Secure – even in trials

In verse 5 of this psalm we are told that God prepares a table for us in the presence of our enemies. It is hard to be sure exactly what this means. Is it that we will eat and drink in the sight of our enemies? That they will, as it were, press their noses against the glass, see us feasting, yet not be part of it?

Or is it that, as the words 'in the presence' suggest, even in the very midst of life's trials we will be succoured and strengthened by God's good provision? The image is almost eucharistic: the table of the Lord set in the midst of the world, a source of nourishment for the soul, protection against evil, and a foretaste of heaven's banquet.

Such a reassurance of God's provision, and such a confidence in God's desire to lavish it upon us (so much, that our cup overflows with God's abundant blessings of goodness and mercy) are therefore as relevant for the beginning of a marriage, and for the birth of a child, as for the ending of a life. God provides for us. He provides for us in life and in death. He is the God of our journeying through life. He is the Divine Shepherd.

Psalm 23 concludes with a hallmark of the psalms – a triumphant echo of praise and confidence in the God who has prepared a place for us: '*Surely goodness and loving mercy shall follow me all the days of my life, and I will dwell in the house of the Lord for ever.*'

QUESTIONS FOR GROUPS

BIBLE READING: PSALM 23 – see p. 16

Some groups will address all the questions. That's fine. Others may prefer to select just a few and spend longer on each. That's fine, too. Horses for (York) Courses!

Please see the suggestion in the box at the bottom of p. 5 about reading the Psalm together.

1. Have you experienced 'goodness and loving mercy' throughout your life?

2. **Re-read Psalm 23.1.** All three participants like this image of God as shepherd (on track 26 of the CD/transcript); Rose thinks it's 'wonderful'. Do you agree with her – is it comforting to know that you are protected and watched over? Or do you feel it is demeaning to be described as a sheep? How would you describe your relationship with God?

3. **Re-read Psalm 23.6.** Do these words encourage you as you go about your daily life? Do you believe them 100%, 80%, 10% – or perhaps wholeheartedly from time to time? What sustains your faith? What might prompt an overwhelming sense of God and his love: a piece of music, a wonderful view, a child's giggle, a powerful sermon … ?

4. **Read Hebrews 10.25 and Matthew 18.20.** On track 28 Timothy reminds us that sheep 'belong to a community'. The fellowship of others in the church is vitally important for every individual Christian – which doesn't necessarily mean that we always get along swimmingly together. Discuss these ideas from personal experience.

5. 'Death is indeed the darkest valley,' says Bishop Stephen. Do you agree? (Tracks 31-32.) For some, death is a merciful release from suffering; so 'assisted suicide' continues to be hotly debated. Where do you stand? Do we have the right to determine the time and manner of our own death – or should we leave this in God's hands? The Gill Pharoah box (p. 18) and Tanni Grey-Thompson box (p.17) might stimulate your discussion.

6. Do you think much about your own dying and/or death? Not just the 'big' questions about what happens next, but the practical stuff like making a will/living will, assigning power of attorney, and perhaps (especially for older members!) planning your own funeral service. What's stopping you if you haven't already done so?

7. **Read 1 Corinthians 15.20-26 and the two boxes at the top of p. 17.** On track 31 John Bell says, 'If you hope in heaven, then there is always hope.' For centuries Christians have drawn strength from the 'hope of heaven'. But modern believers seem less confident about glory to come. How about you?

8. **Read Revelation 21.1-5.** C S Lewis is quoted by our participants. He wrote a book called *Reflections on the Psalms*, and famously believed in heaven, hell, judgement and purgatory. Do you? On tracks 33-5 Rose, Timothy and John give us their views on life in heaven. What do you hope heaven will be like?

9. **Re-read Psalm 23.4.** Have you walked through 'the valley of the shadow of death' yourself, or with some one else? Where did you draw strength from? E.g. friends, neighbours, prayer, church …? Did you draw on this psalm for strength – or on any other passage of scripture?

10. **Read Song of Songs 2.3.** It is often said that while the Victorians were upfront about death, they swept talk about sex under the carpet – and that in the modern western world we do exactly the opposite. Do you agree, and if so is this healthy?

11. Stephen Cottrell says Psalm 23 'speaks powerfully to us today'. Is he right? An archdeacon suggested to his unchurched 21-year-old cousin that she might read Psalm 23 at a family funeral. She was confused – partly by the rustic imagery; secondly by 'enemies' suddenly popping up in the middle. Has Psalm 23 passed its sell-by date for most young people? Does this widespread lack of knowledge about our Judeo-Christian heritage distress you? How might we turn the tide?

Psalm 127

YORK COURSES

the **psalms**

prayers for today's church

UNLESS THE LORD BUILDS THE HOUSE...

> The more I talked with wholehearted Christians at university, and explored evidence for claims in the Bible, the more I realised this world-view made sense of my life.
>
> *Stephanie Bryant, project co-ordinator, God and the Big Bang*

> We are fortunate to have the Bible and especially the New Testament, which tells us so much about God in widely accessible human terms.
>
> *Arthur Schawlow, Nobel Prize-winning physicist*

> When the solution is simple, God is answering.
>
> *Albert Einstein*

> Forgiving means giving up the right to get even.
>
> *John Ortberg, author*

> Two wrongs don't make a right, but they make a good excuse.
>
> *Thomas Szasz, psychiatrist*

Why do we love the psalms?

Is it because they are ancient and venerable, hallowed and refined by countless tongues over hundreds of generations? That is part of the truth. But it is not the whole truth. These words are so alive because they communicate the biblical faith that Jesus learned and fulfilled. Like all prayers, they give voice to the faith itself as well as to the longings of the heart. This is why the psalms are so important. This is why we love them and need them. As we immerse ourselves in them so our life of prayer *and* our life of faith will be renewed and expanded. We will be given words to express our joy, our faithfulness, our frustration, our fears. At our time of need we will have words at hand. And at the same time these very words will expand and enlarge our faith.

The psalms carry passionate conviction, exuberance and joy – not just because of their age, but also because of their youth. Thomas Merton said that in their words *'we drink divine praise at its pure stainless source, in all its primitive sincerity and perfection'.* In other words, the psalms are young. They give voice to the youthful strength and directness of the people of God. This is the reason the psalms endure.

Psalm 127

1 *Unless the Lord builds the house,*
  those who build it labour in vain.

2 *Unless the Lord keeps the city,*
  the guard keeps watch in vain

3 *It is in vain that you hasten to rise up early*
  and go so late to rest, eating the bread of toil,
  for he gives his beloved sleep.

4 *Children are a heritage from the Lord*
  and the fruit of the womb is his gift.

5 *Like arrows in the hand of a warrior,*
  so are the children of one's youth.

6 *Happy are those who have their quiver full of them:*
  they shall not be put to shame
  when they dispute with their enemies in the gate.

Psalm 127 is one of my favourite psalms. I like the reminder that children are a gift from God and a heritage. And the fantastic promise that there will be sleep! Rest in abundance is God's gift to his beloved. But the confident assertion, that without God all our efforts are in vain, is the main reason I find this psalm such a comfort – and a challenge.

It gives a wonderful reminder of the primacy of God. Getting up ever earlier and composing ever more ambitious to-do lists; working longer and faster; staying up half the night doing our emails ... all this is in vain and entirely useless – unless we first acknowledge that God is at the beginning of our labours, that God is the source of life, and that God is the *point* of our labours.

It is God who gives reason and purpose to our every endeavour. It is God who is doing his work through us – even in the tiniest things we do. Without God there is nothing. All our labours are our way of co-operating with God in his endless work of creation. By so doing we praise God, because we participate with God in his great work of 'building his house'. Carried out in this spirit, our work gives pleasure to God. God delights in us. That is why, when we do get things in the right perspective in the way this psalm declares, the reward is a good night's sleep!

Faith brings rest

Many of the great spiritual writers of the Christian tradition have picked up on these themes. Brother Lawrence, an obscure lay brother working in the kitchens of a French Carmelite monastery in the seventeenth century, wrote: *'The time of action does not differ from the time of prayer. I possess God as peacefully in the bustle of my kitchen ... as I do upon my knees before the Holy Sacrament ... I turn my little omelette in the pan for love of God. When it is finished, if I have nothing to do, I prostrate myself on the ground and worship my God who gives me the grace to make it ....'*

This is a gloriously simple example of letting the Lord build the house. Brother Lawrence's daily recitation of the psalms – a keystone of the monastic life – has changed him.

Building with God

The images of 'building' and 'being built' have resonance throughout scripture. The creation itself is God's handiwork (Psalms 8 and 19). In Jesus, God comes to make his home in our home. He empties himself of what it is to be God (Philippians 2.5-11) and makes the womb of the Virgin Mary his dwelling place. Jesus also longs to make his home in every human heart, and for us to make our home in him: 'Abide in me' says Jesus, 'as I abide in you.' (John 15.4.)

Moreover, in one of his most famous stories, Jesus speaks of two houses: one built on sand, the other on rock (Matthew 7.24–27). Come the crisis, the house on the sand collapses. It has no foundation. This story comes right at the end of the Sermon on the Mount, in which Jesus shares that wisdom which is the foundation of the Christian life.

We build our foundations on Christ, who is himself the rock of which the psalms speak.

I love you, O Lord my strength.
The Lord is my rock, my fortress, and my deliverer,
my God, my rock in whom I take refuge …
(Psalm 18.1-2)

Christ the sure Foundation

'The stone that the builders rejected has become the chief cornerstone.' (Psalm 118.22.) The early Church saw this as a direct reference to Jesus. He was the foundation stone, but one that had been rejected by his own people.

We can affirm today that the life, death and resurrection of Jesus, his teaching and his example, are the foundation and the compass for everything that we do. As we go about our daily lives as disciples of Jesus, we know that what we do is the Lord's work and the Lord's will. So we also know that we do not labour in vain.

We may not see the results of our labours. They may often seem mundane. We may think that our discipleship is not up to much. But if we live out of this dynamic of faithfulness, where every deed and action – however small – becomes a participation in God's work of creation and redemption, and becomes a hymn of praise to the creator and redeemer God, then our lives will be fruitful.

God the Builder

I love the imagery of Psalm 127, with its simple and encompassing affirmation that it is God who builds the house, and that we are fellow labourers with him. As the Apostle Paul asserts:

'Each builder must choose with care how to build ... for no one can lay any foundation other than the one that has been laid; that foundation is Jesus Christ' (1 Corinthians 3.10-11).

With all their energy and variety, their honesty and probing, and their incisive imagery, the psalms are, if you like, the bricks and mortars of a Christian life – a source of prayer and praise and the foundation of a spiritual life.

Pray the psalms and the Lord will build the house.

Pause for thought

A man died and St Peter met him at the pearly gates. St Peter said: 'Here's how it works. You need 100 points to make it into heaven. You tell me all the good things you've done, and I give you points for each item. If you reach 100 points, you get in.' 'Okay,' responded the man, 'I worked hard all my life to give my family a happy, secure home.'

'That's great,' said St Peter, 'that's worth one and a half points.'

A bit shaken, the man went on, 'Well, I attended church all my life and supported its ministry with my money and my time.'

'Terrific!' said St Peter, 'that's certainly worth another full point.'

'Only one point?' exclaimed the hapless man, scratching about in his memory. 'How about this then: I started a soup kitchen in my city and worked in a shelter for homeless people.'

'Fantastic, that's good for two more points,' said St Peter.

'TWO POINTS!!' cried the man in dismay, 'At this rate the only way I'll get into heaven is by the grace of God!'

'WONDERFUL!' responded St Peter, 'You've hit the jackpot. Come on in! Welcome to the exciting life of heaven.'

From 'Lord ... Help my Unbelief' by Canon John Young

QUESTIONS FOR GROUPS

BIBLE READING: PSALM 127 – see p. 20

BIBLE READING: PSALM 127 – see p. 20

Some groups will address all the questions. That's fine. Others may prefer to select just a few and spend longer on each. That's fine, too. Horses for (York) Courses!

Please see the suggestion in the box at the bottom of p. 5 about reading the Psalm together.

1. **Read Philippians 2.12-13 and Colossians 1.29.** The old adage declares that, *'God helps those who help themselves.'* Does he? (Track 39 of the CD/transcript.) In contrast, Psalm 127.1-3 seems to suggest that God helps those who leave it to him – as in the saying *'Let go and let God'.* Which of the sentiments in italics do you identify with?

2. **Read the two boxes about sleep on p. 22.** This psalm seems to encourage us to slow down. Is this sensible, or even possible? Do you sleep well? Any tips for insomniacs?

3. **Read 1 Corinthians 15.58.** This psalm addresses two vital areas of life: work and family. Many people complain of busy-ness and stress. We used to be told that labour-saving devices would mean we would all have much more leisure. It never happened. How can we all slow down? Can we defeat the tyranny of the urgent – so that we can focus on the really important?

4. **Read the words about Brother Lawrence on p. 21.** Paula Gooder has written a book called *Everyday God*, whereas John Bell (track 46) prefers 'God everyday'. Which term best describes *your* God?

5. **Re-read Psalm 127.6.** In today's world 'a quiver full' of children might be viewed as irresponsible. Worldwide population growth raises immense questions for sustaining life of a tolerable quality for everyone: environmental issues, water shortage/possible water wars, famine … Pope Francis talks about 'responsible parenthood' adding that 'three children seems about right'. Comments please.

6. 'I like the reminder that children are a gift from God and a heritage' says Bishop Stephen on p. 21. But many who wish for a child are not granted that gift. These days, the talk is of a woman's 'right' to have a child – how do you feel about this? Should infertility treatment be funded by the National Health Service?

7. **Read Ephesians 6.1-4.** Many churches cater for families. Does your church? And how are single people welcomed in to the life of your church?

8. **Read 2 Timothy 3.16.** As we draw near to the end of this course on the psalms please reflect on how/whether this ancient book called the Bible still provides guidance for us in our modern world. On BBC Radio 4's *Desert Island Discs* some people refuse to accept the offer of a Bible – presumably because they are atheists, and possibly because they believe the Bible to be harmful: sexist, anti-gay, pro-war … Our participants defend the Bible against such charges on tracks 43-44. Is what they say helpful?

9. A young relative challenges you: 'Our world is so different from the world inhabited by the psalmist well over 2,000 years ago. How can anything written then 'speak' to us today?

10. Is there a topic arising from this course you would like to raise or revisit?

If you've found this course challenging or helpful, you might want to do another one. It might be a good idea to decide on a date to start, before you end this last session.

You choose whose thoughts and ideas you'd like to listen to and discuss in your group ...

We have an extensive list of ecumenical courses, suitable for any time of year – including Lent and Advent. All are ideal for discussion groups, and suitable for individual reflection. The majority of our courses have 5 sessions, but there are 4- and 6-session courses too, and the range is growing every year.

THREE 4-SESSION COURSES

The course CDs feature the course author in relaxed conversation with Canon Simon Stanley. With input from churchgoers, together they explore the themes raised by the course booklets.

Making Room ...

... for the newcomer; the stranger; what really matters; for God

Life is full of things to do, people to see, responsibilities and chores. We can sometimes feel there's not enough time or space in our lives for the people and things that really matter – including God. **Revd David Gamble** uses New Testament stories to help us consider why and how we might make room for what really does matter.

JESUS: the voice that makes us turn
Course booklet by Bp David Wilbourne

A four-session course, reflecting on Jesus' many voices.

A Crying Voice homes in on the baby's cry at Bethlehem, announcing that God was in town. *An Other Voice* focuses on the strangeness of Christ, whose command stilled the storm, forgave sins and raised the dead. *A Dying Voice* sees new depths for living in Jesus' familiar words from the cross. *A Rising Voice* examines the immense quality that made downhearted disciples turn and fire the world with their faith.

Four different voices that will make us turn in our tracks and say to Christ, 'I want you!'

EXPECTING CHRIST

Course booklet by Bp David Wilbourne

The writer Graham Greene famously said that there is always one moment in childhood where a door opens and lets the future in.

In this course we look at several moments in our faith and lives where a door opens and lets Christ in, catching the sense of expectancy which not only comes at the season of Advent, but throughout the year.

In particular, we think about how Christ can surprise us and meet us in four distinct contexts: in family, in ourselves, in prayer and in the end.

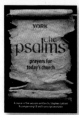

THE PSALMS

Course booklet written by Bishop Stephen Cottrell

The ancient poems we call Psalms were written when humans travelled at the speed of a camel – not at the speed of sound. But these songs have stood the test of time for they address many of the problems we still face: violence, injustice, anger – and bewilderment. Why do the wicked prosper? Where is God when we suffer? This course reflects on the psalms in general (and five psalms in particular).

With Fr Timothy Radcliffe, Revd Preb Rose Hudson-Wilkin, Revd John Bell, and Revd Dr Jane Leach.

PRAISE HIM
songs of praise in the New Testament

Course booklet by Dr Paula Gooder

This course explores five different Songs of Praise from the New Testament – what they tell us about God and Jesus, but also reflecting on what they tell us about ourselves and our faith.

With Archbishop Justin Welby, Sr Wendy Beckett, David Suchet CBE and Moira Sleight.

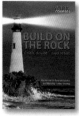

BUILD ON THE ROCK
Faith, doubt – and Jesus

Is it wrong – or normal and healthy – for a Christian to have doubts? Is there any evidence for a God who loves us? We hear from many witnesses. At the heart of a Christian answer stands Jesus himself. We reflect upon his teaching, death, resurrection and continuing significance.

With Bishop Richard Chartres, Dr Paula Gooder, Revd Joel Edwards and Revd David Gamble.

GLIMPSES OF GOD
Hope for today's world

Course booklet by Canon David Winter

We live in turbulent times. This course draws on the Bible, showing where we can find strength and encouragement as we live through the 21st century.

With Rt Hon Shirley Williams, Bishop Stephen Cottrell, Revd Professor David Wilkinson and Revd Lucy Winkett.

HANDING ON THE TORCH
Sacred words for a secular world

Worldwide Christianity continues to grow while in the West it struggles to grow and – perhaps – even to survive. What might this mean for individual Christians, churches and Western culture, in a world where alternative beliefs are increasingly on offer?

With Archbishop Sentamu, Clifford Longley, Rachel Lampard and Bishop Graham Cray.

RICH INHERITANCE
Jesus' legacy of love

Course booklet by Bp Stephen Cottrell

Jesus left no written instructions. By most worldly estimates his ministry was a failure. Yet his message of reconciliation with God lives on. With this good news his disciples changed the world. What else did Jesus leave behind – what is his 'legacy of love'?

With Archbishop Vincent Nichols, Paula Gooder, Jim Wallis and Inderjit Bhogal.

WHEN I SURVEY...
Christ's cross and ours

Course booklet by Revd Dr John Pridmore

The death of Christ is a dominant and dramatic theme in the New Testament. The death of Jesus is not the end of a track – it's the gateway into life.

With General Sir Richard Dannatt, John Bell, Christina Baxter and Colin Morris.

These three...
FAITH, HOPE & LOVE

Based on the three great qualities celebrated in 1 Corinthians 13. This famous passage begins and ends in majestic prose. Yet it is practical and demanding. St Paul's thirteen verses take us to the heart of what it means to be a Christian.

With Bp Tom Wright, Anne Atkins, the Abbot of Worth and Professor Frances Young.

THE LORD'S PRAYER
praying it, meaning it, living it

In the Lord's Prayer Jesus gives us a pattern for living as his disciples. It also raises vital questions for our world in which 'daily bread' is uncertain for billions and a refusal to 'forgive those who trespass against us' escalates violence.

With Canon Margaret Sentamu, Bishop Kenneth Stevenson, Dr David Wilkinson and Dr Elaine Storkey.

CAN WE BUILD A BETTER WORLD?

We live in a divided world and with a burning question. As modern Christians can we – together with others of good will – build a better world? Important material for important issues.

With Archbishop John Sentamu, Wendy Craig, Leslie Griffiths and five Poor Clares from BBC TV's 'The Convent'.

WHERE IS GOD...?

To find honest answers to these big questions we need to undertake some serious and open thinking. Where better to do this than with trusted friends in a study group around this course?

With Archbishop Rowan Williams, Patricia Routledge CBE, Joel Edwards and Dr Pauline Webb.

BETTER TOGETHER?
Course booklet by Revd David Gamble

All about relationships – in the church and within family and society. *Better Together?* looks at how the Christian perspective may differ from that of society at large.

With the Abbot of Ampleforth, John Bell, Nicky Gumbel and Jane Williams.

TOUGH TALK
Hard Sayings of Jesus

Looks at many of the hard sayings of Jesus in the Bible. His uncomfortable words need to be faced if we are to allow the full impact of the gospel on our lives.

With Bishop Tom Wright, Steve Chalke, Fr Gerard Hughes SJ and Professor Frances Young.

NEW WORLD, OLD FAITH

How does Christian faith continue to shed light on a range of issues in our changing world, including change itself? This course helps us make sense of our faith in God in today's world.

With Abp Rowan Williams, David Coffey, Joel Edwards, John Polkinghorne and Dr Pauline Webb.

IN THE WILDERNESS

Like Jesus, we all have wilderness experiences. What are we to make of these challenges? *In the Wilderness* explores these issues for our world, for the church, and at a personal level.

With Cardinal Cormac Murphy-O'Connor, Archbishop David Hope, Revd Dr Rob Frost, Roy Jenkins and Dr Elaine Storkey.

FAITH IN THE FIRE

When things are going well our faith may remain untroubled, but what if doubt or disaster strike? Those who struggle with faith will find they are not alone.

With Abp David Hope, Rabbi Lionel Blue, Steve Chalke, Revd Dr Leslie Griffiths, Ann Widdecombe MP and Lord George Carey.

JESUS REDISCOVERED

Re-discovering who Jesus was, what he taught, and what that means for his followers today. Some believers share what Jesus means to them.

With Paul Boateng MP, Dr Lavinia Byrne, Joel Edwards, Bishop Tom Wright and Archbishop David Hope.

CD CONVERSATIONS

In addition to discussion courses we also produce **CD Conversations** featuring leading Christian thinkers, **books** and **booklets**. A selection of these is shown below to whet your appetite.

Please visit **www.yorkcourses.co.uk** where detailed information on the full range is available, and you can listen to sound bites from the CDs, and view sample pages from our course booklets and transcripts.

JOHN BELL
Hymn writer and author John Bell of the Iona Community talks about life, faith and music.

WHY I BELIEVE IN GOD
Oxford philosopher and Anglican priest Prof. Keith Ward sets out his reasons for believing in God.

HAWKING DAWKINS AND GOD
Revd Dr John Polkinghorne KBE FRS, an Anglican Priest and Fellow of the Royal Society, discusses his Christian faith in the light of the New Atheism and explains why he believes in God.

ROWAN REVEALED
The 104th Archbishop of Canterbury talks about his life and faith, prayer, the press, politics, the future of the Church ...

CLIMATE CHANGE AND CHRISTIAN FAITH
Nobel Prize winner Sir John Houghton CBE, FRS, a world expert on global warming, talks about why he believes in Climate Change and in Jesus Christ.

Transcripts are available for most of our CD Conversations. CD Conversations available as multi-packs at www.yorkcourses.co.uk

---

PAPERBACKS by CANON JOHN YOUNG

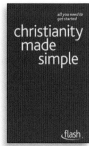

Lord... Help my unbelief
"John Young is an outstanding communicator of the Christian message"
(Canon David Winter)

Christianity – an introduction
"An exciting, engaging and intellectually serious book"
(Archbishop Rowan Williams)

Christianity made simple
A short and to-the-point guide to Christianity, set out in just 96 pages.

PARTICIPANTS ON THE COURSE CD:

- **FR TIMOTHY RADCLIFFE** OP is Director of the Las Casas Institute, Blackfriars, Oxford and an itinerant preacher and lecturer. He was a Trustee of the Catholic Agency for Overseas Development from 2001 to 2014. He was awarded the Michael Ramsey Prize for theological writing in 2007.

- **REVD PREBENDARY ROSE HUDSON-WILKIN,** BPhil Ed was born and grew up in Montego Bay, Jamaica. In 2007 she was appointed as a Chaplain to Her Majesty the Queen and in 2010, she became the first female Chaplain to the Speaker of the House of Commons.

- **JOHN BELL** is a Resource Worker with the Iona Community, who lectures, preaches and conducts seminars across the denominations. A hymn writer, author and occasional broadcaster, John is based in Glasgow and works with his colleagues in the areas of music, worship and spirituality.

- **REVD DR JANE LEACH** is the Principal of Wesley House, Cambridge, having previously served as a Circuit Methodist Minister. She has published articles and books on theological education, pilgrimage and pastoral supervision, and is a regular broadcaster on Radio 4's *Thought for the Day*.

THIS COURSE BOOKLET is written and introduced by Bishop Stephen Cottrell, who was consecrated as Bishop of Chelmsford in 2010. Before ordination he worked in the film industry, and for a year at St Christopher's Hospice in Sydenham. A longstanding member of the Governing Body of the College of Evangelists, he is the author of numerous books.

For more information about some of the matters raised in this course, visit www.yorkcourses.co.uk

---

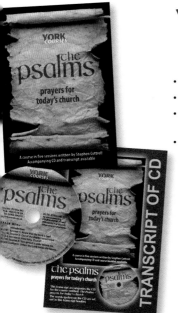

YORK COURSES

- founded in Lent 1997
- widely used in Britain and throughout the world
- committed to ecumenical activity and to honest exploration, sharing and deepening of faith
- Produced by Simon Stanley (Canon of York Minster and former BBC producer/presenter) and John Young (best-selling author).

Canon Simon Stanley   *Canon John Young*   *Elaine Stanley, Administrator*

A FIVE-SESSION COURSE

for groups and individuals - for Lent or any season

Featuring on CD
- **Bishop Stephen Cottrell** *(Introduction)*
- **Fr Timothy Radcliffe** OP
- **Revd Preb Rose Hudson-Wilkin**
- **Revd John Bell**
- **Revd Dr Jane Leach** *(Closing Reflections)*

See inside this cover for details of the participants

THE PSALMS
prayers for today's church

This **BOOKLET** accompanies the CD

FIVE SESSIONS:

1. Know that the Lord is God
2. Out of the depths have I cried
3. How long, O Lord?
4. You spread a table before me
5. Unless the Lord builds the house…

A word-by-word **TRANSCRIPT**
of the CD is also available.

'York Courses really do offer some of the best material for group use, attractively presented, ecumenical, and not tied to a particular season.'
Church Times reviewer

ISBN 978-1-909107-10-6

York Courses · PO Box 343 · York
YO19 5YB UK · Tel : 01904 466516
email: courses@yorkcourses.co.uk
www.yorkcourses.co.uk

YORK
COURSES

SAVINGS ONLINE AT www.yorkcourses.co.uk